Rosalind Ca[...] Washington, with her husband, James, and children, Steve and Sharon. She has written more than fifty articles, one hundred short stories and thirteen books.

Rosalind attempts to write about "real" people, rather than creating characters. She's also an avid researcher. For *Lovespell*, she herself visited many places in the story.

Books by Rosalind Carson

HARLEQUIN TEMPTATION
40–LOVESPELL

HARLEQUIN SUPERROMANCE
16–THIS DARK ENCHANTMENT
40–SONG OF DESIRE
91–SUCH SWEET MAGIC
123–LOVE ME TOMORROW

These books may be available at your local bookseller.

Don't miss any of our special offers. Write to us at the following address for information on our newest releases.

Harlequin Reader Service
P.O. Box 52040, Phoenix, AZ 85072-2040
Canadian address: P.O. Box 2800, Postal Station A,
5170 Yonge St., Willowdale, Ont. M2N 6J3

"I shouldn't have dropped by."

As he spoke, Michael settled himself more comfortably on the bed with Blythe. "But I missed you while you've been sick," he added quietly.

"You have?" she whispered, gazing up at him. The tenderness in his voice made her heart skip several beats.

"Very much." He leaned over and kissed her lips gently. One hand strayed to her breast, teasing the nipple beneath the sheer fabric of her nightgown.

Blythe felt herself sliding into the honeyed pleasure of sweet passion. Once more, Michael had begun weaving his sensual spell around her....

Lovespell

ROSALIND CARSON

Harlequin Books

TORONTO • NEW YORK • LONDON
AMSTERDAM • PARIS • SYDNEY • HAMBURG
STOCKHOLM • ATHENS • TOKYO • MILAN

This book has to be for
my friend George Glay

Published December 1984

ISBN 0-373-25140-8

Printed in Canada

BOUGAINVILLEA CASCADED over the high walls of the courtyard, so brilliantly scarlet against the light-colored adobe that Blythe was almost blinded when she looked down at the wedding party on the terrace steps.

It was a blessing to see sunshine after the two weeks of storms that had buffeted San Diego's shores. The good weather wasn't accidental, of course. According to Julie, the bride, her mother had ordered it specially from the wedding consultant she'd hired. "Sunlight is absolutely essential for an outdoor Valentine's Day wedding," Julie had quoted, rolling her eyes and giggling as she imitated her mother's rather pompous tones. "How else can we be sure the lipstick red of the bridesmaids' dresses will contrast effectively with my daughter's white-veiled loveliness and the groom's and best man's sober black?"

The best man. Blythe flinched inwardly. No, she wasn't going to look at the best man.

Julie and Russell had exchanged their rings, she noted. The minister was leaning forward, covering their clasped hands with his. It was time for Blythe to sing.

She looked over her shoulder at her twin brother, David, saw that his right hand was poised over his guitar strings and stepped forward to the microphone, feeling the slim skirt of her ivory silk dress slide sensuously against her long legs, making her feel self-conscious. Nervously she checked with one hand that her honey-colored hair was neatly tucked into its usual French braid.

There was a moment's silence, then a ripple of chords from David's guitar. Julie had asked Blythe to write a song for this special moment, and she had been delighted to do so. Though she wasn't completely satisfied with the result, she wanted to put all the expression and beauty she could into her singing—her gift for Julie and Russ.

She had sung the first section before she noticed that Julie was desperately trying to extricate her hand from Russ's and the minister's so that she could wipe tears from her eyes. Pausing while David played, she saw the bridegroom reach into his tuxedo pocket for a handkerchief and pass it discreetly under his bride's veil. Blythe suppressed a smile, glad Russ had come prepared. In spite of her merry, sometimes irreverent attitude to life, her old schoolfriend Julie obviously wasn't immune to the solemnity of her own wedding.

Russ's eyes were also suspiciously moist. The bridesmaids were tearful. Moved herself, Blythe let her voice rise on the next stanza to its clearest register.

A moment later, as she sang, "Now and forever, two become one," she happened to glance at the best man. *His* eyes were totally dry. Narrowed. Admiring. A smile hovered around one corner of his mouth. She was suddenly sure he had been watching her for some time in that same narrow-eyed manner, as though he were an artist patiently sizing up a composition he intended painting, a composi-

tion that secretly amused him in some way that was
not apparent to other people.

For one heart-stopping moment, Blythe's breath
caught in her throat and she faltered. Then disci-
pline took over and she continued smoothly, hoping
no one had detected the catch in her voice. Unfortunately, now that she'd caught the best man's gaze,
she was unable to look away.

How dark his eyes were. She had noticed them
earlier, when the groom had hurriedly introduced
her to him just before the ceremony. They didn't
shine like other people's. They gleamed, giving him
a slightly devilish air that was matched by his
crooked smile. She'd thought even then that his
smile seemed too intimate, too knowing, and had
felt a swift surge of embarrassment. She also remembered thinking he had the type of build tuxedos and
frilled white shirts were designed for. He looked at
home in the formal clothing, not at all stiff and self-
conscious like Russ and every one of the ushers. He
was fairly tall, six feet one or two, with a tough yet
slender body that looked as though it could move
around a tennis court without any problem, a shock
of blue-black hair that might have been impatiently
finger-combed into place and an appealingly wry
face—all planes and angles—with straight, dark eyebrows that slanted upward above a strong nose.

No doubt about it, he was an attractive man, with
an air of careless elegance about him. But she had
seen attractive men before. What had disturbed her
earlier—and disturbed her even more now—was the
blatant sexuality that seemed to surround him like
an aura, a sexuality being telegraphed to her as
clearly as though he were standing there naked.

There was another pause while David played. Blythe seized the opportunity to take a deep breath, desperately striving for her usual composure. Why was he staring at her as though they shared some kind of secret? She hadn't met him before today, she was sure of that. Was he in the navy with Russ? He surely didn't look like any sailor she'd ever seen. He might be an actor, she thought—she could imagine him playing 007, casually piling chips on a roulette table, one hand in the pocket of his dress trousers; or a diamond thief who burgled only the best houses. How had Russ introduced him? Michael somebody, a roommate from university days. So he'd be Russ's age...thirty-five or so. Ten years older than Blythe...ten years more experienced. He *looked* experienced. Dangerous.

As she began to sing again, his dark gaze shifted a little, lazily moving down her body, then back to her face. He was still smiling faintly, intimately, as though he found her particular combination of tall slim figure, light-brown eyes and blond hair to be...delectable. To her dismay, her body was responding with primitive stirrings. This was insanity. He was making love to her with his eyes, in public, and she was allowing him to do so. Dry-throated, aware that her heartbeat had increased and was pounding in her ears, Blythe glared fiercely at him, then forced her gaze away to her boyfriend, Craig, who was seated on a folding chair among the guests on the bride's side of the courtyard, separated from the groom's friends and relatives by an elegant fountain.

Craig was smiling up at her with obvious pride, looking attractively muscular in his charcoal-gray suit. He'd had his light-brown hair trimmed the previous day in the usual neat style that complimented his tanned even features and made him look slightly older than his twenty-eight years. He'd have looked quite the man-about-town had it not been for the damp gray shine of his eyes.

Another sentimental idiot, she thought lovingly, feeling relieved that she'd managed to recover her poise. Several handkerchiefs were being used surreptitiously, she noticed. The bride's mother was openly sobbing, though Blythe wasn't sure if the song had moved her or she was expressing her sorrow over the match. A submariner, even if he was an officer and certainly a gentleman, was not quite the husband Mrs. Wallace had wanted for her beloved but rebellious daughter.

Abruptly, involuntarily, Blythe's gaze was brought again to the best man. He was staring even more boldly, relentlessly. As she sang the final words of the song, Blythe felt a pulse start up in her throat. Her fingers were trembling and heat was spreading through her whole body. Embarrassment, she wondered. No, not embarrassment. Awareness. *Sexual* awareness.

"YOU WERE TERRIFIC," her brother told her as the guests crowded around the bride and groom. He grinned at her, his fair-skinned face with its high cheekbones a mirror of her own except for its mischievous expression. "There wasn't a dry eye in the house."

"Yes, there was," Blythe murmured, but not loud enough for David to hear.

Blythe was soon surrounded by guests herself, all of them extravagant in their compliments. She thanked them as calmly as she could, while all the time she was wondering frantically if they could see the pounding of her heart under the clinging silk of her gown. She was afraid, she realized, terrified that the best man would approach her, would speak to her as outrageously as he had stared at her.

She wished Craig hadn't disappeared so soon after she'd descended to the courtyard. He'd been hauled off by the flower girl, Julie's precocious twelve-year-old sister, to view the wedding cake, a heart-shaped, triple-tiered confection that had been wheeled out on a serving cart by one of the household servants. David was occupied, too, flirting with Stephanie Goodwin, a pleasantly plump brunette who was one of Julie's bridesmaids. Stephanie was studying David's rangy body and curly blond hair as though she had never seen anything quite so miraculous before. Romance was in the air—not an unusual phenomenon at a wedding.

A bevy of men hired for the occasion were setting up a buffet table and rearranging the chairs in groups here and there. Yet in spite of the bustle and the attention being showered on her by those around her, Blythe knew the precise moment when the elegantly lean man began to shoulder his way easily through the throng.

"Your voice should be classified as a secret weapon," he said when he reached her. He wasn't smiling, but his well-educated voice had a mocking edge to it. The people around Blythe laughed. Then the group broke up, as though the man's intimate tone had warned them away.

"Is that supposed to be a compliment?" Blythe asked. The words emerged with an ease that surprised her. This man had such a bewildering effect on her she'd half expected her voice to quaver. The pulse in her throat had begun beating wildly again.

"It certainly is. You do realize you reduced everyone to tears?"

"Except for you," she responded tartly, taking refuge in sarcasm.

"I was too enthralled to cry. But I must admit your voice reached right inside me and twisted my heart." He laughed shortly. "I'd forgotten I had a heart. Thank you for reminding me." He hesitated, but there was nothing hesitant in the way he looked at her. "You have a very clear, pure voice," he added slowly. "Perhaps that's the problem."

"There's a problem?" Blythe was surprised again at the cool tone of her voice. Chaos was rampant inside her. Close up, the man's dark gaze had an almost hypnotic intensity. She couldn't look away, and fiery little darts of sensation were playing havoc with her nervous system. God, this man had charm. No, that wasn't an apt word. Charm didn't include overtones of self-mockery. Charisma? Too overworked. Vitality? Magnetism? Or just good-old sex appeal?

His fingers reached to touch the pulse that was still beating in her throat. Aware that she should quell him with a few well-chosen words, Blythe could only stand helplessly, willing her body not to tremble, which it showed a distressing inclination to do.

"The pure part, I mean," he said at last, smiling. "Somehow you managed to move everyone with the poignancy of your voice, but the words themselves didn't have quite the emotional impact they should have. Especially the part about two people becoming one. I know you wrote the song, but I have an idea you haven't experienced that particular phenomenon."

With an effort, she moved back a step, away from

his hand. "I don't know what you're talking about," she said.

"That's exactly what I mean," he answered with a knowing smile. There was a small curved line at one corner of his sensual mouth, like a misplaced comma. She had an almost irresistible urge to trace it with her fingertips. What was happening to her?

"You're a friend of Russ's, aren't you?" she said, hoping some small talk would dissipate the extraordinary tension between them. "Are you a submariner, too?"

"No."

She waited for him to go on, to explain who or what he was, but realized at last that he wasn't going to make anything easy for her. How was it that she seemed to know instinctively what he was thinking?

She tried again. "I don't believe I caught your full name?"

Anyone else would surely have supplied his name at once. But not this man. He lifted her left hand in his, bent over it and gazed at her palm. "I'm something of a fortune teller," he informed her. "Strictly amateur standing." His thumb rubbed lightly, intimately over her palm, sending electrical impulses racing through her bloodstream. "The lines in the left hand are an indication of the past and the possibilities of the future. Did you know that?" He didn't wait for an answer. "Obviously you were a very solemn child. People told you that you had a good head on your shoulders. You always did what your parents told you to do. It looks as though you never gave them a moment's worry."

The analysis was so close to the truth that it took her a minute to think up a light-enough answer. But before she could speak, he picked up her right hand and smiled into her eyes. "Here, however, we see changes coming. See the little loops on your lifeline?"

"Surely you aren't going to tell me I'm about to meet a tall, dark, handsome stranger," Blythe said flatly.

His smile was whimsical as he straightened, releasing her hands. "You think I'm handsome? Thank you."

She laughed, but her hands felt empty. She didn't quite know what to do with them. "You were going to tell me your name?" she managed.

He didn't hesitate this time. "I'm Prince Charming, of course," he said evenly. "Don't tell me you didn't recognize me? I'm here to awaken you from your hundred years' sleep and take you off to my castle to live happily ever after."

It was such an impossibly hackneyed approach that Blythe couldn't stop herself from smiling. "What makes you think I've been sleeping?" she asked lightly.

The line bracketing the corner of his mouth deepened. "No one who'd ever been properly awakened could look so virginal."

Blythe swallowed. This was going too far. The problem was that she had no idea how to answer him. Such outspokenness was beyond her experience. She could hardly tell him she wasn't a virgin, which had been her first wayward impulse.

"I don't believe in fairy tales," she got out at last.

"I know." His voice was grave, but his eyes danced with light, and those impossibly slanted eyebrows of his had lifted perceptibly. "I intend to change that," he said, then added surprisingly, "Would you like to dance?"

Blythe stared at him. "'Dance'?" she echoed stupidly.

He nodded and inclined his head sideways, indicating the lower courtyard. Blythe realized then that the small combo Julie's parents had hired had begun playing and several couples were indeed dancing together down there. "I haven't congratulated Julie and Russ yet," she objected. "And I have to find my boyfriend. Craig. Craig Foster. He was here just a minute ago...."

Ignoring her stammered excuses, the man took her elbow in one warm, subtly caressing hand and eased her toward the stone steps. "One, the bridal couple is occupied with photographs," he pointed out. "And two, if your boyfriend had any sense at all, you wouldn't have to look for him—he'd be glued to your side like a shadow."

It seemed safest to ignore his last remark. "Shouldn't the best man be in the photographs?" she asked.

"I've already done my duty. I will reappear at the cutting of the cake, ready to ogle the maid of honor as custom demands. For now, no one appears to need me, and I want very much to dance with you. It's the best excuse I can think of to get you in my arms."

They had somehow reached the foot of the steps. Blythe looked at him, startled once again. He returned her glance levelly, and she hastily averted her eyes as his arm came around her.

He was a superb dancer. That didn't surprise her. She had an idea this man would be superb at anything he wanted to do. She seemed to fit perfectly into his arms and was immediately conscious of the iron strength of the shoulder beneath her left hand, the firm warmth of his right hand at her waist. He didn't allow her to hold his other hand away from their bodies in proper dancing style, but pulled her hand close to his body and trapped it against his chest, so that she could feel his heart beating steadily beneath his black tuxedo and ruffled white shirt. She followed him with ease, though he was taller than her by a head. Several other people glanced at them as they moved slowly in time to the music, and she heard a woman say softly, "My, how handsome they look together, Michael and the girl who sang."

"Blythe Sherwood," Michael murmured into her hair. "An enchanting name. Conjures up visions of blithe spirits and Sherwood Forest. Merry men pursuing Maid Marion."

Blythe laughed at the whimsical image and was rewarded by a smile of approval. "That's better," he said. "You are much too serious, Blythe Sherwood."

"Life is serious," she said in a deliberately profound voice.

He groaned and pulled her closer. "Only if you make it so," he told her.

And then he lapsed into silence and concentrated on moving her with him to the music. The music had changed to a soft, insinuating beat, a tune she didn't recognize, something vaguely South American. She was aware of his body from head to toe, almost aware of the blood flowing through his veins. Knowing she should pull away from his close embrace, she found herself instead leaning against him, letting the music enter into her, her heart beating in time to the soft throbbing of the drums. She felt weightless, as if her feet barely touched the ground. And now Michael's fingers were pressing against her back, burning through the thin silk of her gown, causing her breathing to become uneven, her throat to close.

"I think perhaps we should..." she began tentatively, lifting her head from his shoulder, where it had somehow found itself a comfortable niche.

"Ssh," he murmured. "Don't break the spell, or we'll all disappear for another hundred years."

She accepted his wish for silence, so intrigued by this man that she was beginning to wonder if she could have been affected by the champagne Julie's parents had provided, but which she had not yet touched. Could someone become drunk on just the sound of champagne corks popping, she wondered. Could the sparkling bubbles have turned the air to wine? Certainly she was not acting like herself— levelheaded, sensible, practical Blythe.

She seemed to be sealed away from the other guests in a magic bubble, enclosed with this disturbingly attractive man in some other dimension where reality had ceased to exist.

Yet strangely, her senses were heightened rather than dulled. She could see the brilliance of the bougainvillea, smell the perfume of the other women around her and the occasional sharp odor of a cigar, hear the shuffle of shoes on the stone courtyard and the endless, repetitive beat of the drums.

"We've met before," Michael told her.

"We have?"

His fingers were still pressing so firmly against her spine that she wondered if there would be marks later on her fair skin. His other hand was clasping hers tightly, and now he raised it to his lips. She felt the touch of his mouth on her fingers, butterfly tender, reverberating down to her toes.

"In some faraway land and time. England, perhaps. Two characters in Tennyson's "Idylls of the King." Arthur and Guinevere? We danced in the castle courtyard to the music of the gentle evening breeze, with a harp thrown in for added interest." He laughed softly. Then his lips grazed her fingers again. "Camelot," he added. "In the moonlight."

Their joined hands pressed intimately against her breast, but Blythe didn't seem to want to protest. Without any apparent effort, he had drawn her willingly into the scene he'd so vividly created. Mesmerized by his low voice, she had become part of his fantasy and made it her own.

"When the music ended," he continued softly, "we went to our castle bedroom and I coaxed you into freeing your golden hair from that so-practical braid. When it tumbled around your shoulders as nature meant it to do, I lifted the silken weight of it in both my hands, and then I kissed that mouth of yours that looks as though it were made for kissing, so sweet and gently curved it is. And then we danced again until the sun rose and set and rose once more."

The music stopped and people applauded. Yet Blythe seemed unable to move. They were both standing very still, and he was looking at her as if he could see all the way inside her. For just a moment—one magical moment—she could smell the breeze he'd mentioned, hear pennants fluttering, feel the touch of his lips on hers.

Craig's stiffly smiling face suddenly loomed up beside Michael's. His hand touched Michael's shoulder. "May I cut in?" he asked politely, and she realized the music had started again.

Michael released her at once, and she stumbled, disoriented by the abrupt transition from fantasy to reality. Craig's hand reached to support her. "Have you been drinking?" he asked in a disbelieving tone of voice.

Blythe swallowed and glanced sideways at Michael, feeling totally unstrung. Somehow she managed to look back at Craig. "Of course not," she said faintly, wondering what on earth had happened to her in the past few minutes. Had she slept on her feet? Had she dreamed?

No. That strange interlude had not been a dream. The line at the corner of Michael's mouth had once again deepened perceptibly. He was standing very straight and tall, looking at her challengingly, his dark gaze excluding Craig.

She found herself remembering something altogether irrelevant. During the first two years she and David were in college, before their double tragedy had made it necessary for them to give up frivolous pastimes, they had studied fencing. She was reminded now of the moment when the opponents take the "on guard" position, both bodies poised for action. What action there would be in *this* situation she had no idea.

With an effort, Blythe forced her gaze back to Craig. And saw that his usually clear gray eyes were the slaty color of a stormy sea. At once the strange spell of enchantment dropped away.

"I'm sorry, Craig," she said hastily. "I couldn't find you, and everyone seemed busy, and Mr. er, Mr.—"

"Charming," Michael supplied under his breath.

"That isn't really your name," Blythe objected.

"Channing, then, if you insist."

The name sounded familiar. Where had she heard it before? Shaking her head in an effort to clear it,

Blythe murmured, "Thank you for the dance, Mr. Channing. If you'll excuse us?"

"Of course."

She wouldn't have been surprised if he had bowed from the waist and kissed her hand, but instead he gave her a funny sort of salute that made her wonder again if he was one of Russ's navy colleagues. Then he turned abruptly and strode toward the steps. Blythe watched admiringly, even while she was turning into Craig's arms, expecting him to dance with her.

Craig's muscular body was rigid. "What the hell were you doing with that man?" he demanded.

She glanced at his face, surprised. Craig wasn't usually possessive. It was one of the things she appreciated, *loved* about him. And he was never jealous. Though of course she hadn't ever given him reason to be jealous.

"You were plastered against that...that gigolo like a piece of wallpaper," Craig said as she continued to look at him blankly.

The remark struck her as funny. "Is he really a gigolo?" she asked, laughing.

"Well, maybe he doesn't get paid for his services," Craig admitted grudgingly. "But he's forever changing women, and they're usually older than he is, with each one richer and more beautiful than the last. He has a new one every week." He paused. "You know who he is, don't you?" he added grimly. "He owns all those restaurants, five or six of them at least. Chez Michel, The Dockside, Michael's On The Pier...."

That Michael Channing. Of course. No wonder his name had sounded familiar. She'd pointed out his restaurants to tourists countless times.

"You must have read about his divorce," Craig continued. "It was in all the papers a couple of years ago."

She didn't remember. Why should she?

"She divorced him," Craig said. "I met her once at a party. Ellie. A really sweet woman, kind of innocent. That's why it bothered me when you—"

"I'm sorry, Craig," she said softly. "You're quite right. He did hold me too close and he was much too suggestive. I won't dance with him again."

Craig relented at once, smiling at her. "I'd offer to deck him for you, but he looks as though he'd be pretty fast on his feet. He might even carry a knife—he looks the type."

"*I* thought he looked as though he could play 007," Blythe said, laughing. "Or maybe a Mississippi riverboat gambler. I guess it isn't fair of us to jump to conclusions about him, though. He's probably a very respectable citizen. He's a friend of Russ's, after all." She paused. "Speaking of Russ, shouldn't we pay our respects to the bride and groom?"

Craig nodded, and they walked up the steps together. Julie and Russ were beginning to cut the cake. They were surrounded by the wedding party, but the best man was nowhere to be seen. Had he left already? Why should that thought distress her? She wasn't distressed, she scolded herself. She was merely surprised. He should be there, posing for the photographs with the others. In fact, she could hear Julie asking Russ where he'd gone. Probably he'd appear at any moment and smoothly take his place at the maid-of-honor's side.

But he didn't come. It was over an hour before Blythe saw him again. Then he was suddenly hovering on the edge of the crowd of guests as they pressed close to the bride, demanding that she throw her bouquet. He was watching her—Blythe, not Julie—with a quizzical expression that seemed natural to him.

Deliberately Blythe turned her back toward him. Whatever had happened to her in his arms, she wasn't about to repeat the heady experience. She was forewarned now, aware of the effect this devastatingly attractive man could have on her. Aware enough to avoid him at all costs. She didn't need someone like him in her well-ordered life.

There was a sudden squeal of laughter as Julie tossed her bouquet over her shoulder. She had thrown it too high, and it bounced off one edge of the stone fountain and was fielded deftly and automatically by Michael Channing. He looked at it bemusedly for a moment as everyone applauded. Then he straightened. Oblivious to the amused glances that followed him, he marched straight toward Blythe, his dark eyes holding her spellbound in their direct, compelling gaze. No, she thought, panic-stricken, feeling Craig stiffen on one side of her, David on the other. He couldn't plan on giving it to her. He couldn't possibly do such a—

He was in front of her, eyebrows raised in that disturbing inverted vee. "For you, Sleeping Beauty," he murmured.

Even though she was desperately embarrassed and beginning to be furious, there was no way she could avoid accepting the proffered nosegay. Not with all those people watching, laughing, exclaiming.

"Thank you," she said in a falsely gracious voice. Turning to Craig, she smiled brilliantly at him and took his arm. "Maybe we should get married right away," she suggested gaily. "Think of the money we'd save on flowers."

She saw him grin and heard David laugh and turned triumphantly toward Michael Channing, expecting to find him chagrined by her unexpected poise. Instead she was met by a loving, understanding gaze that unnerved her so totally the bouquet almost slipped from her suddenly trembling hand.

"We'll dance again," he said quietly, so quietly that neither Craig nor David seemed to hear. But Blythe heard, and she knew without any doubt at all that he had spoken the truth.

2

BLYTHE AND DAVID'S PARENTS had died five years previously, when the captain of their rented yacht, encouraged by his passengers, had disregarded the storm warnings that had been clearly posted and had ventured too far from Pago Pago in rough weather. The yacht had capsized, leaving no survivors.

It had often seemed to Blythe that her parents' deaths had been symbolic of the way they'd lived. Sailing happily through life, madly in love with each other, refusing to worry about anything, they had insisted, in spite of John Sherwood's erratic income as a realtor, that they and their children wear only clothes created by top designers, dine only on gourmet foods accompanied by imported wines. They had charmed their way into the hearts of all who knew them, including their two children, constantly missing disasters such as bouncing checks, repossessed furniture or even possible bankruptcy by the breadth of a hair no wider than any on their handsome blond heads. "If you spend your life expecting a storm, you can't enjoy the sunshine," Jennifer Sherwood had often declaimed.

Blythe, who had been born practical, according to her mother, had sensed something too hedonistic, too selfish in this philosophy even while her parents were alive, and she'd found a certain irony in it, in spite of her mind-numbing grief, when it became apparent that all the Sherwoods had left their twins were memories of two beautiful people, a house that was mortgaged to its last wrought-iron gatepost and a staggering array of past-due bills. She had coined a new Sherwood slogan the day reality hit her: "You can't enjoy the sunshine unless you're prepared against the storm."

Determined to finish college, David and Blythe had faced the necessity of working for the first time in their lives. The tour business had been Craig's idea. He and David had been experienced tour guides even before they graduated from the University of California. He'd recommended both Blythe and David to the tour company he worked for, but unfortunately his employer had decided that as the majority of tourists were female, the guides should be male. Blythe had managed to find a series of odd jobs, delivering pizza, free-lance accounting, singing occasionally at weddings and parties. The last two years at school had been a real struggle, but they'd made it, largely due to Craig's help. Not having had their advantages, he'd already been skilled at drawing up budgets and sticking to them, at buying good clothes in bargain basements of better stores, at creating nourishing soups out of vegetables in season.

By the time David and Blythe received their diplomas, Craig had worked out the details of the business they would share and had arranged for financing by a banker uncle. Many people avoided tours, he'd discovered, because they didn't like the herd concept. Why not, then, provide a fleet of minibuses that would carry no more than fifteen people? With this concept, Wanderlust Tours had been born.

The "fleet" had begun with one bus and had recently expanded to include one more. The three of them took turns either driving or working in their tiny office, which was squeezed in between two boutiques on the Embarcadero, San Diego's historic and popular waterfront strip.

"Better to be in an accessible spot," Craig had decreed, "even if it means having less space."

They expected to buy one more bus this year, which would necessitate employing another driver. Having to pay someone else's social security, Blythe felt, would mean they were firmly established in business. Already they had each discovered their strengths. David, as a history major, delighted in learning as much as he could about their tour area and sharing his knowledge with their clients. Craig, who'd majored in business and management, was their senior partner. Blythe, who'd planned to major in music but had hastily switched to business herself, kept the books in impeccable order, but also took her turn as guide because she enjoyed the break from office routine.

Several days after Julie's wedding, she was describing to an elderly couple from Indiana, who had walked over after lunch in the nearby Holiday Inn, the various tours Wanderlust offered. Carl and Vera Schmidt, both round and short and gray haired, were having a difficult time deciding if they wanted to venture into Mexico, or not. "We've traveled a lot," Carl told Blythe proudly, "but we haven't gone out of the good old U.S. of A. before. Mother and me, we wouldn't want to get mugged, or anything."

Having assured them they'd be as safe in Tijuana's colorful bazaars as in their own supermarket, Blythe was going on to describe the first half of the all-

day tour, when she had the spine-tingling feeling
that she was being watched. Turning sideways to
look through the plate-glass window that faced the
Embarcadero, she saw Michael Channing standing
under the palm tree outside, smiling in at her, his
blue-black hair shining in the sun, his tall body imprinted like a double exposure on the reflection of
her own blue cotton overblouse and light gray skirt.
Beyond him, across the street, soared the tall masts
and bare rigging of the *Star of India*, the old wind-
jammer that was now a maritime museum. The man
might just have disembarked from the ship—a bold
buccaneer looking for amusement in port.

Something about the combination of images sent
heat flooding through her. The heat of annoyance,
she assured herself as she hastily averted her eyes.
He had been standing very still, looking directly at
her, and there was something about his posture—a
patience—that indicated he'd been watching her for
some time.

As Carl and Vera peered over their spectacles at the
brochure Blythe had spread open on her desk, she
glanced again at the window. No one was there. But
before she could explain to her own satisfaction the
feeling of disappointment that washed over her, the
door opened and Michael came in, seeming to bring
with him an odor of fresh sea breezes that overrode
the office's sometimes unreliable air-conditioning.
He looked every bit as rakish and darkly attractive in
a tan safari shirt and well-pressed slacks as he had in a
tuxedo. Giving her a quizzical smile that made every
corpuscle in her bloodstream come to attention, he
took up a position in front of the tubs of brilliant yellow chrysanthemums opposite her desk, folded his

arms across his chest and fixed his dark gaze on her face.

"I'll be with you in a few minutes, sir," she managed.

He nodded without averting his gaze.

Evidently his entrance had rattled Carl and Vera almost as much as it had affected her. As though afraid the arrival of a new customer threatened their chances of getting space on the next day's tours, they started arguing again about the wisdom of risking the wilds of Mexico. "Would you just describe the Tijuana trip one more time?" Carl asked.

Patiently Blythe did so, though she had to refer to the brochure herself a couple of times. She felt jittery. Michael Channing's presence was having an effect on her brain cells as well as her bloodstream, and she couldn't seem to concentrate. Why didn't he turn around and look at the flowers or the posters on the wall, as most customers who were forced to wait would do? Didn't he know it was rude to stare?

The collar of his safari shirt was open, showing the beginnings of a thick mat of dark hair.

Where had all the air gone, she wondered, feeling irritated. The sea breeze effect of his entrance had dissipated. He seemed larger than life; his presence filled the tiny room. She could feel a film of perspiration on her upper lip and her hands felt clammy. What was he doing here?

After more agonizing minutes of deliberation, it occurred to Carl to ask who would be driving them on the tour. When Blythe assured him she would be conducting them herself, he gave her a very sweet smile, pulled out his wallet and counted out the necessary amount.

"We will have lunch in the U.S.?" Vera asked anxiously as Blythe made out a receipt.

Blythe managed another smile. "At the Hotel del Coronado," she assured Vera. "You'll love it, it's a marvelous old place, all turrets and cupolas and Victorian gingerbread. Elisha Babcock, one of the men who built the Coronado, came from Indiana," she added as the happy thought occurred to her.

That was enough for Vera.

As soon as the door closed behind the now-eager old couple, Michael seated himself in the chair opposite her desk that Carl had vacated. "Isn't this a happy coincidence!" he exclaimed.

"'Coincidence'?" Blythe echoed warily.

"Finding you here." He stretched out his long legs and leaned back, smiling at her in a way that seemed to invite her to share his pleasure.

"I can't think how many times I've passed your office and promised myself I'd come in," he said airily. "If I'd known the proprietress was my princess in disguise I'd have galloped in on my white charger the day you opened." He gave her a deliberately suggestive smile, then followed that up with a solemn expression that was just as contrived. "Makes you believe in fate, doesn't it? Meeting you at the wedding, then running into you here, makes it obvious that—"

"Why are you here?" Blythe asked before he could go off into another flight of fancy.

The question earned her an admiring smile. "So businesslike," he approved. Then he leaned forward, all business himself. "I'm here to book a tour, of course."

"For yourself?"

"Why so disbelieving? Do I appear so jaded that I

can't possibly admire the beauties of my own surroundings? Admittedly I've left it rather late. But
I've decided it's high time I looked more closely at
my own little corner of the world, widened my
scope, so to speak."

Blythe could think of no one whose scope seemed
less likely in need of widening, but she managed not
to say so, asking instead, "You just happened to pick
on Wanderlust Tours?"

His Indian-dark eyes gazed at her with deceptive
innocence. The comma-shaped line beside his mouth
deepened. "Not at all. It was recommended to me. I
can't stand crowds."

"That's why you're in the restaurant business, I
suppose?"

He grinned appreciatively, but didn't comment.

"We have several tours," she said briskly. "One to
the zoo, Sea World, the Wild Animal Park—"

"How about the city tour that ends up in Tijuana?"

"You've never been to Tijuana?"

"There's that disbelieving tone again. I've never
gone as a tourist. There's a world of difference, I understand. And I believe your tour stops off in Old
Town before crossing the border. It would be good
for me to see it through a tourist's eyes, I think."

"Good for you?" Even as she queried him, she remembered that one of his restaurants was in the Ba-
zaar del Mundo, part of the restored Old Town that
was now a state park. "Did you have a particular
date in mind?" she asked. "We run that tour on
Tuesdays and Thursdays."

"It's Thursday tomorrow."

There was a glint in his dark eyes that was beginning to unnerve her. "You didn't really just happen
to come in here, did you?" she accused.

He grinned wickedly, then spread both palms in a gesture of surrender. "I confess. I asked Julie where I could reach you without running into either of your stalwart bodyguards. She told me about this place and said that if you were in the office, brother and boyfriend would be otherwise engaged."

"You can't have talked to Julie. She's on her honeymoon in Puerto Vallarta."

"I asked her on her wedding day. I've looked in here every day since, but was unrewarded until today. Here you are, so here I am."

"Why?"

A devilish expression appeared on his lean face. With a sudden and totally unexpected movement he leaned across the desk and lightly touched her cheek with the tips of his fingers. It was the most intimate gesture imaginable. "Surely that's obvious," he said.

For a split second she gazed at him wordlessly. Then she drew away from his hand as though his touch had burned her. Somehow she managed to recover her brisk office voice. "I'm afraid I don't have either the inclination or the time for...."

"Dalliance?" he suggested when she ran out of words. He nodded solemnly. "I realize you work very hard. Julie told me how devoted you are to your business."

"We all are. David and Craig and I." She put extra emphasis on Craig's name, and he looked amused.

"Ah, yes, Craig...Foster, is it? He seems like a nice boy."

"He's hardly a 'boy.'" She rushed on as his amusement obviously deepened. "All I meant was that it would be a waste of your money to take a tour if you thought that I would be...had any thoughts of...." She was floundering again, and he made no effort to help her, instead keeping his amused gaze on her face in an intent way that made her throat dry up and words fail her.

"But I *want* to take the tour," he insisted.

"I'm not sure there's a vacancy."

"Now, now, Blythe. Is that any way to treat a prospective customer?"

Flustered in spite of her resolve not to be, Blythe pulled the scheduling journal toward her and glanced at it, knowing full well there were three vacancies left. "I guess I can fit you in," she said reluctantly.

"I thought you might be able to." Glancing at the brochure, he wrote out a check and passed it across to her, then pocketed his receipt. "Pick up outside the Holiday Inn?" he asked.

She nodded. "Or one of the other hotels, whichever is most convenient." She averted her eyes as she suddenly thought of a way to get out of accompanying him.

"I would suggest you don't decide to switch with one of your cohorts," he remarked lightly, reading her mind. "I'd just have to cancel and keep trying until I get the guide of my choice."

"But there's no point," she said evenly, managing to meet his teasing brown eyes directly.

He sighed audibly. "You're determined to make this difficult, aren't you?" His smile was slightly crooked now, rueful. "It won't make any difference, you know. I enjoy a challenge."

She was suddenly as exhausted as though she'd gone through a particularly rugged fencing match. It was necessary to put this man in his place once and for all. "I suppose if you have nothing better to do, you might as well waste your time playing games." She was proud of the disinterested note in her voice.

He was smiling. Didn't anything faze him? "So cool," he said admiringly. "So perfectly in control." He laughed shortly, leaning forward. "Blythe Sherwood, you really are absolutely, impossibly—"

"I've been told often enough by men of your type that I'm unapproachable, Mr. Channing," she said angrily. "I don't need to hear it from you!"

In her agitation, she had stood up and knocked her receipt book to the floor. He bent to pick it up as she crouched to do the same. His head barely an inch from hers, he asked softly, "What type am I, Blythe?"

"A—a philanderer." She felt foolish using such an old-fashioned word, but it was the one that had come to mind.

Those impossible eyebrows quirked upward. "How dreadful it is to be constantly misjudged," he said. Then he straightened, looking down at her. "I was about to say that you are absolutely, impossibly beautiful and I don't remember when I've ever wanted any woman as much."

Awkwardly she pulled herself up and sat down again, looking at him uncertainly, totally bereft of words. Inside her something moved, like the feathery brush of a palm branch in a light breeze, a movement that was almost imperceptible but somehow heralded a storm. The feeling terrified her.

"The minute I saw you, I knew you were going to matter to me," he continued earnestly. "You stood straight and slim as a candle in your ivory dress, every hair on your head in place and shining pale gold in the sunshine. Ethereal. I'll admit that I saw you as cool and unapproachable at first—you put up a barrier the moment Russ introduced you to me—

but then you sang, and something in your voice woke an echo in my beat-up old heart."

He grinned suddenly. "And then you glared at me because I was staring, and I caught a glimpse of fire under the ice that intrigued me even more." He hesitated again, his eyes narrowing. "I guess I want to see if I can ruffle that perfection."

Once more he leaned across the desk, standing now, and again touched gentle fingers to her cheek. "I'll see you tomorrow," he said.

And then he moved toward the doorway, pausing when he reached it. Looking back over his shoulder, he said very seriously, "You shouldn't wear pale blue, you know. Not pale anything. You should be surrounded by bright colors, like the gold at the end of the rainbow."

BLYTHE HAD EXPECTED that Craig would be annoyed when he discovered the next morning that Michael Channing had signed up for a tour, but she hadn't expected him to be furious. "He's obviously marked you down as his next victim," he said heatedly as he leaned over the desk, reading the day's schedule. "The man's a shark, a barracuda."

She sighed with exasperation. Ever since Michael Channing had come into their lives, the usually imperturbable Craig had been acting like a jealous husband. Evidently there was something about Michael that sparked his enmity.

In the next instant she chided herself for pretending ignorance. Quite obviously Craig had sensed the turmoil Michael Channing created inside her. Naturally he would feel threatened by it. Michael was so...different. Poised, sophisticated. And arrogant, her mind added. Though Craig was better looking, no one could describe him as sophisticated. Handsome, yes, especially when he wore the sharply creased gray slacks and gray and blue T-shirt with the Wanderlust logo that he was wearing today. There was an attractive neatness about Craig's appearance always, a well-put-together look, whatever he was wearing. And the Wanderlust colors suited him far better than her. She hated to agree with Michael Channing, but he was right in this instance.

"We'll be well chaperoned," she said lightly.

"Ha."

It wasn't like Craig to be sarcastic. Annoyed, she turned away toward the mirror that hung on the back wall of the office, tucking a few stray hairs into her usual French braid, remembering to her chagrin the sound of Michael's caressing voice when he had talked of holding the silken weight of her hair in his hands, remembering too that he'd told her she was absolutely impossibly beautiful. Which she certainly wasn't. She'd admit to good bones—she'd been told often that she had the look of a high-fashion model—and she rather liked the fact that she possessed brown eyes with blond hair—which wasn't too common—and her figure was slim enough—too slim, if the truth be told. She retied the sash of her blue overblouse and smoothed the cotton fabric over the hips of her gray skirt, then smiled up at Craig in the mirror as he put his hands on her shoulders from behind. "Don't let's quarrel," she said. "Michael Channing could just want to take a tour."

Craig grinned at her, his burst of temper gone as quickly as it had arrived. "Don't try to fool me into thinking you're naive, Blythe Sherwood," he said lightly. "I know better."

She smiled fondly at him in return. "Okay," she admitted. "It looks as though Michael Channing has designs on me. But he's a paying customer, and he's done nothing to give us the right to refuse to take him."

"Has David left on the first zoo trip already?"

She nodded.

"I could take the Tijuana run."

"I don't think...." She hesitated. As well as she knew Craig, she wasn't sure how he'd react if she passed on Michael's threat to postpone his trip if such a change was made. There was no sense in asking for problems. "I'm quite capable of handling Michael Channing," she said instead.

In the mirror, Craig's gray eyes clouded. For a moment he seemed to be thinking deeply. Then he said, "I'm not so sure you can." He nodded briskly. "I'll take over for the day. It's a hot one, anyway. You'll be better off in the office."

"I said I could handle him," she repeated, turning away from their joined reflections.

He gave her a coaxing smile and slid his arms lightly around her waist. "Come off it, Blythe. Don't go independent on me."

There was a patronizing note in his voice that annoyed her. She stood rigidly in the circle of his arms, not softening when he lightly nuzzled her throat, even though she felt an answering warmth to his touch. And then he added, "I could make it an order, you know. I am the senior partner in this enterprise."

She pulled herself free, glaring at him. "You've never pulled rank before."

His smile had faded. "I've never had reason to before."

"Well, it won't work. I'm scheduled to drive this tour. I promised the Schmidts I would. And I'm going to."

"Michael Channing turns you on, doesn't he?"

For a split second she hesitated, and Craig's eyes narrowed. But before he could protest again, she gathered up her purse and headed for the door.

"We'll talk about this later," Craig added.

Sighing, she looked back at him, forcing her irritation away. He was standing very straight, looking impossibly handsome but grimmer than she'd ever seen him. Why on earth was she fighting with him about Michael Channing? She'd even thought herself it would be a good idea to switch tours. "Michael Channing isn't of enough importance to me to make him worth discussing," she said softly. "I'll admit there's something about him that's very attractive. And he makes me laugh. But he doesn't affect me...that way."

The lie caused Craig's muscular body to release its tension. "It's just that I...I care about you, Blythe."

"And I care about you." Would Craig ever get around to saying, "I love you," instead of using euphemisms, she wondered. He surely knew by now that she wasn't out to trap him into marriage. She was quite content with their relationship the way it was. They had become lovers nearly two years ago, and while their affair wasn't always passionate, it was warm and comfortable and...yes, caring. They had even talked of marriage, jokingly, as something that might possibly happen in the future. However, neither of them was in any hurry to take that final step.

He smoothed his already-neat hair in a characteristic gesture, then met her eyes, smiling in his usual affectionate way. She laughed. "What a fuss about nothing," she said lightly. "I'll see you later, okay?"

"Dinner?"

"With David and me. I'm cooking tonight. Lasagna."

"The way to my heart."

Laughing, she opened the door and went out into the heat of the morning, glad that she and Craig had been able to part on amicable terms. But her smile faded as she rounded the corner and saw Michael Channing leaning against the side of the silver-and-blue minibus, apparently engrossed in admiring one of the clumps of vivid orange-and-purple bird-of-paradise flowers planted at the edge of the parking area.

"Passengers are supposed to be picked up at the Holiday Inn or one of the other hotels," she reminded him crisply.

He smiled easily, straightening, looking very relaxed in white chinos and a black knit shirt with short sleeves that hugged his upper arms. "I thought I'd save myself a few steps," he said. "I'm inclined toward laziness. You should know that about me before we go too much farther."

Evidently he was going to continue as before. Blythe decided at once she wasn't going to let herself be drawn into another fencing competition. "Okay," she said. "I'll make a note of that." She took a deep breath, then made a face. "It's hot, isn't it? It looks as though the breeze isn't going to show today."

Moving briskly, she unlocked the door of the minibus, gestured him in, then slid it closed behind him. As she might have expected, he took the seat next to hers. He looked at her challengingly as she unlocked her own door, but she didn't comment as

he obviously expected her to do. Nevertheless, she
was very conscious of his gaze on her as she started
the bus and swung the steering wheel. Ducking her
head against the sparkle of sun on water as she eased
out into traffic, she saw Craig standing in the window of the office and knew he'd seen Michael with
her. She couldn't read his expression in the brief
glimpse she had of it, but she was pretty sure he
wasn't smiling.

It's only one day, she told herself grimly as she
pulled up in front of the Holiday Inn. By the end of
it, she'd have convinced Michael Channing he was
not about to add another scalp to his list of con-
quests, and then she could relax back into her usual
well-ordered, serene life.

Unfortunately, even as she thought this, Michael
favored her with a wicked sidelong smile that turned
her bones to jelly and her brain to mush, and she had
a premonition that the day was going to be even more
difficult than she'd imagined.

FOR SEVERAL REASONS—occasional delays at customs,
the length of the drive, the increased heat—the run
to Tijuana was not one of Blythe's favorites. She pre-
ferred the shopping tours of La Jolla and Seaport
Village or the trip to the Wild Animal Park. But she
always conscientiously tried to give her clients a
good time, and she did enjoy rattling off the history
of San Diego as they drove along the Embarcadero,
into the Gaslamp Quarter, Balboa Park and up to the
Cabrillo Monument.

She had an interesting busload: a trio of rather
leathery-faced women from New Zealand; a pair of
incredibly young honeymooners from Paris, who
were spending a month traveling around California;

the Schmidts, who were wearing matching flowered shirts and white pants; and four elderly women from Oregon, who said they'd recently become interested in birds. And Michael Channing.

He didn't have much to say during the early part of the drive, though he did clear his throat as she explained the restoration project in the Gaslamp Quarter, an area of downtown San Diego filled with handicraft stores, antique and art galleries. She remembered then and told her group that one of his restaurants was located there, as well as the one they could visit in Old Town and the others on the Embarcadero and in Seaport Village. The Schmidts were visibly impressed and from then on treated him as a celebrity, which he accepted without noticeable humility.

Her difficulties began soon after that, when she started forgetting things. Though she was not quite as stuffed with information as Craig and David, she was usually fairly knowledgeable. Yet when the Parisian girl asked about the architecture of the California Tower in Balboa Park, she wasn't able to remember what it was, and Michael had to tell the girl it was Spanish-Moorish, which Blythe knew. As she also knew later but couldn't remember, when one of the Oregon women asked if those were cormorants on the rocks. When she listed the major industries of the area for Mr. Schmidt's benefit, she forgot to include electronics and barely remembered to mention the current troubles of the tuna industry.

By the time they reached the top of Point Loma, where they all posed for photographs in front of the monument to Juan Rodriguez Cabrillo, she was simmering with anger, at herself as well as Michael Channing. Even there, though she managed to compose herself enough to point out various sights in the panoramic view of San Diego Harbor, she completely forgot to mention that Cabrillo was the Spanish explorer who discovered San Diego Bay while looking for the always-elusive shortcut to China, and one of the New Zealanders had to ask her who he was.

Craig would have had a fit if he'd heard her. Wanderlust Tours prided itself on its ability to provide copious information. Once or twice she caught Michael glancing at her in his quizzical way, and of course that made her even angrier, especially when he started volunteering information about the navy and the submarines in the fleet—he knew the exact number—and the harvesting of kelp, not to mention the approximate cost of houses they passed—which made Vera Schmidt gasp and decide she and Carl were better off living in Indiana.

In Old Town, a place that vividly recreated California life of the Mexican and early-American periods, he took everyone off for a glass of wine in his restaurant, Casa de Miguel, telling them he'd also escort them on a walking tour of the adobe buildings and quaint shops. Blythe elected to stay with the bus. She needed time to pull herself together.

She sat in the bus beside a riotous bed of pink and orange impatiens, watching her group straggle past Squibob Square, all of them hot on the heels of the lean dark man who had set himself up as a modern version of the Pied Piper. Michael Channing was the sole reason for her intermittent amnesia, she admitted to herself. But even though the problem was his fault, he was hardly to blame. He hadn't really done anything deliberately to annoy her. Occasionally he had glanced at her sideways under those slanted eyebrows of his; once or twice his hand had brushed her shoulder as he pointed out something to the Schmidts, seated behind her, but he could hardly be held accountable for her tense, nervous reactions.

She'd come prepared to be rattled, she realized. After the wedding she'd admitted to herself that he had affected her strongly, physically. Like a frightened rabbit, she'd decided she'd have to avoid him. Then when he'd more or less forced his company on her, she'd become too agitated, afraid of what he might say or do, not trusting her own good sense. From now on she was going to be a model tour guide, with her mind on business and nothing else.

There was one more difficult moment during lunch at the Hotel del Coronado. She had a long discussion about the picturesque, castlelike structure, in French, with the Parisian couple, who were apparently more fascinated by architecture than anything else. She informed them that the exuberantly Victorian hotel had been constructed of wood between March 1887 and February 1888, a time when San Diego had neither lumber nor skilled carpenters. Both were brought in, at great cost, mainly from San Francisco. The hotel's 399 original rooms were still in existence, although every room had been renovated and many more had been added.

After some time, she switched to English. "Edward, Prince of Wales, is said to have met Wallis Simpson here," she told the group as they gazed in awe at the crown-shaped lighting fixtures hanging from the great pegged-and-domed sugarpine ceiling. "And ten United States presidents have visited this hotel: Harrison, McKinley, Taft, Wilson, Eisenhower, Kennedy, LBJ, Nixon and Carter."

"That's only nine," Michael volunteered, causing the New Zealanders to giggle.

"And FDR," Blythe added, fixing Michael with a

look that should have melted him into his gazpacho. "The Crown room seats a thousand people easily," she went on.

"Which is okay unless you hate crowds," the irrepressible man beside her murmured. She faltered for a moment, but rallied and went on to detail the movies that had been filmed at the Del, as the hotel was affectionately known.

She was relieved when they finished their tour of the hotel's lower-lobby shops, poolside terrace and lovely curving beach and were all back on the bus, headed down the Silver Strand to the border. Once she got everyone to Tijuana she could turn them loose for an hour to shop in the assortment of Spanish-style shops and modern international stores. And she knew from experience that on the return trip most tourists were too tired to ask any more questions.

Unfortunately Michael Channing refused to be turned loose. "How about a beer?" he suggested as everyone else piled out.

"I don't drink while I'm driving. I'll be having coffee, but you are free to go shopping or do whatever else you have in mind."

That unfortunate double entendre earned her another wicked glance. But then he shook his head. "I don't do well at haggling, I'm afraid. I see the poverty and I don't have the heart to talk the shopkeepers out of half their profit."

As Blythe felt exactly the same, she could hardly argue with him and she even found herself awarding him points for his sensitivity. However.... "I suggest you find a *taberna*, then."

He nodded, but when she rounded the bus to lock it, he was waiting for her on the sidewalk, grinning

at the swarm of Mexican children who'd immediately surrounded him with hands outstretched.
Some of them were openly begging, others offering
chewing gum for sale. *"Por favor,"* they shouted.

Blythe distributed quarters all around.

"You'll have them in your pocket all the time
you're here," Michael warned.

She shook her head. "We have an agreement," she
said. "They watch the bus for me and leave me alone
and they get another quarter each when I come out."
She spoke in Spanish to the children, reminding
them of their agreement, and they laughed and nodded in chorus.

"Twelve children. Six dollars for an hour's parking. Expensive, some might even say exorbitant,"
Michael commented.

"It isn't the parking, Michael. They have little
enough."

He nodded, ruffling the hair of the boy nearest
him in an affectionate way that made it obvious he
liked children. She felt herself softening toward him
and deliberately stiffened her resolve. He probably
liked dogs, too. That didn't mean he wasn't dangerous to her peace of mind.

He was smiling at her now. "You finally broke
down and used my first name," he pointed out.

She swallowed. "It slipped out. Don't let it give
you any ideas."

"I don't need anything to give me ideas."

Blythe sighed and looked in the direction the
others had taken, thinking she might follow them
after all. Through the crowds, she could see Vera
Schmidt buying a bunch of huge brightly colored
paper flowers from one of the Mexican women who
thronged the insistently commercial Avenida Revo-

lución; the Parisian girl was looking into a store that sold leather goods, with her baby-faced husband already reaching for his wallet; the New Zealand ladies were posing for photographs with one of the sombrero-topped burros. She'd given them her set speech about the conversion of pesos into dollars, the best way to decide on a fair price for anything and customs regulations about plants, but she knew if she joined them they'd have her doing all the mental work for them and it was just too hot. The sun shone brightly on the curio shops and the wide dusty street, hurting her eyes. And she *was* thirsty. "There's a *hostería* at the end of this block that I usually go to," she said, surrendering. "You can get beer there."

"*Carta Blanca, por favor,*" Michael told the waiter as he seated them.

The waiter nodded and glanced shyly at Blythe with velvety brown eyes as she ordered her coffee. "*¿Cómo le va?*" he asked her.

"*Muy bien, gracias,*" she told him. Very well. "*¿Y usted?*" And you?

He nodded, smiling broadly, and went off to get their order. "Spanish and French," Michael said approvingly. "How many languages do you speak?"

"Only those." Blythe sat back in the basket-weave chair and closed her eyes momentarily, enjoying the plant-laden, shaded coolness of the *hostería* and the mingled scents of *chili relleno* and *chorizo* and spice. From the busy street outside she could hear the sound of traffic and raised voices and a mariachi, but they all seemed muffled and far away.

Michael didn't respond, and she opened her eyes to find him studying her, an expression on his face that she could only interpret as wounded. She had sounded rather terse, she supposed. She could at least be reasonably polite. "I'm thinking of studying Japanese," she told him with a smile. "Craig once went to Japan with a tour group, and he was impressed by the fact that so many hotel and tour employees spoke excellent English. We should do more for visitors here, he decided, so we all brushed up on French and Spanish and hope to gradually acquire more languages."

He nodded, but the strange expression hadn't left his face. "Why do you dislike me, Blythe?" he asked.

Luckily the waiter arrived with their drinks and she had a moment to compose an answer. The coffee was hot and very black, revivifying. "I don't dislike you, Michael," she said crisply. "It's just that you come on too strong. And you took my tour away from me."

"I see." His mouth quirked. "Made you mad, did I?"

"You could say that."

"Well, that's better than leaving you indifferent. But I don't really want to antagonize you. I thought I was being helpful. You seemed rather...distracted." His dark eyes narrowed thoughtfully. Then a wry smile lit his lean tanned face and his gaze met hers with a raking intensity that stilled her breath and made chaos of her thinking processes. "A change of tactics is called for, obviously," he murmured.

"No 'tactics,'" she began, but she was interrupted by the arrival of a pair of children who had evidently come to entertain the patrons of the *hostería*. The boy was about eight, sturdy and healthy, wearing blue jeans, T-shirt and a sombrero almost as big as he was. The little girl, probably his sister, was no more than five, wearing a pink rayon dress. The boy carried a guitar. Neither of them wore shoes.

The boy's playing was surprisingly skilled, but both piping voices were a little off-key. Everyone applauded just the same, and the boy took off his sombrero and went around collecting. Michael waved a twenty-dollar bill at him and he approached rapidly, eyes fixed on the money.

Blythe protested. "You were the one who accused me of overpaying."

Michael smiled benignly, one arm around the boy's shoulder, his other hand still holding the bill. "I have a special job for them to do," he explained. Bending down, he beckoned the little girl close and whispered to both children for some minutes, to Blythe's growing curiosity. When the colloquy was over, the children swapped a conspiratorial glance with their potential benefactor and then looked expectantly at Blythe.

"I've told them you'd like the boy to play again so you can sing," Michael said.

"I'm not going to do anything of the sort," Blythe said hotly.

The children's large dark eyes were still fixed on her. "No song, no money for them," Michael said.

"You couldn't be so cruel," she protested.

"You hold the remedy in your hands." He grinned. "Perhaps I should say in your throat." He leaned forward, smiling, directing the full force of his eyes and charm at Blythe, making her feel at once weak in the knees and yet strangely filled with power.

She remembered his voice saying, "I've never wanted any woman as much." She could see the desire on his face, implicit in the sensual gleam in his dark eyes, the soft curve of his mouth, the persuasive intensity of his body language as he leaned toward her, one hand pressing gently on her knee.

"Humor me please," he murmured. "I desperately want to hear you sing again. You aren't shy about singing, are you? You sang to all those wedding guests."

"That was different." She forced her gaze away from his face and glanced at the children, then couldn't look away from their eyes. The boy had evidently followed most of the conversation and was now staring dolefully at the twenty dollar bill as though he suspected he wasn't going to come into unexpected riches after all. "Oh, all right," Blythe said wearily. "I shouldn't give in to blackmail, but I'll never sleep tonight remembering those eyes."

The money transferred itself to the boy's jeans pocket with the speed of light, and he began strumming the guitar, smiling at Blythe now, his expression changed instantly from sorrow to anticipation. She had the feeling she'd been thoroughly conned. But she couldn't help laughing all the same.

"'*Vaya Con Dios*,'" she told the boy, then picked up the little girl and seated her on her lap. The children hummed along as she sang but didn't attempt to sing themselves.

There was a great deal of applause when the song was finished, not only from the *hostería* patrons, but from a small crowd of onlookers who had gathered on the sidewalk outside. Responding to requests for more, she sang "*Estrallita*" and then "*Bésame Mucho*," amused by the increasing flamboyance of the boy's playing. The little girl snuggled warmly in her lap, and Blythe couldn't resist kissing the petal-soft cheek before releasing her. Michael smiled at her warmly as though he approved her gesture.

"Did you ever think of singing professionally?" he asked after the children left, the boy clasping one hand over his jeans pocket.

Still bemused by the music and the charm of the children, Blythe answered honestly. "I used to dream about it. Fantasizing, you know?" She was silent for a moment, caught up in the memory of how desperately she'd once wanted to pursue a career in music. Even now she occasionally felt a yearning. . . .

She became aware that Michael was watching her closely, that her expression must have mirrored her thoughts. There was sympathy in his eyes and understanding. For a second she was tempted to say more, to tell him of the time when she was a little girl and had watched a Judy Garland show on television— probably twenty years ago—on which Barbra Streisand had sung, and how she'd dreamed of becoming one or the other of the two passionate and dramatic singers; how even after she was older, she'd visualized herself standing on a stage, mesmerizing people with the beauty and power of her voice.

Her usual good sense came to her rescue. "Apart from weddings and parties there's not much call for a voice like mine," she said briskly. "I had to face the fact years ago that it's not big enough for opera or musical comedy."

"You could sing with a group. There's a unique sound to your voice that's very appealing, poignant."

She shook her head. "Few people can make an adequate living from singing. It's too erratic, chancy. You have to be really talented to get anywhere."

"You're perfectly happy guiding tours?"

She frowned. "I enjoy it. And we have plans for expansion. Eventually we'll have others doing the legwork. Craig thinks we can employ someone else this year if everything continues to go well."

"This Craig of yours," he said abruptly. "Where exactly does he fit in?" He was looking pointedly at her ring finger.

"We're sort of unofficially engaged," she said, thinking even as she spoke that she should be more precise. Her voice had sounded...uncertain. "We're very close," she added.

"How long has this unofficial engagement gone on?"

She smiled reminiscently, feeling on much safer ground. "I've known Craig since high school. He was a couple of years ahead of David and me, and I hero-worshipped him, I guess. But he didn't really notice me in school. He was more David's friend." She hesitated. "He was wonderful to me when I needed him. When my parents died he took care of practically everything."

"And now you have your life together all planned out?"

"Yes." That was better, she'd sounded more confident.

He sighed deeply. "I guess I'm going to have to save you from yourself, Blythe Sherwood."

"I don't need saving," she said crisply. "I know exactly where I'm going."

He cocked an eyebrow and she half expected another caustic comment, but instead he said thoughtfully, "I knew your father slightly. He sold me some land—the site of Chez Michel. A charming man. He seemed to enjoy life more than most. He didn't strike me as much of a planner, though."

"No, he wasn't." She couldn't prevent a tinge of bitterness from coloring her voice, and he looked at her questioningly. But she didn't explain, and after a moment he diplomatically changed the subject, asking her if she'd eaten at any of his restaurants. She had several times and complimented him on the food and the service. "How did you get started?" she asked, suddenly curious. "You must have worked very hard."

He looked offended. "Me, work? Perish the thought." He laughed, reminiscent in his turn. "I was the family bad boy. Never really interested in school, though I did all right. Mostly I clowned a lot—which made my father furious. Still does. My father is a lawyer. My two older brothers are lawyers. I was supposed to become a lawyer, too. I didn't have the courage to tell dad I hated the thought, so I dropped out of law school in my senior year and got a job hustling pool. I wasn't very good at that, either, so I washed dishes on the side. One day a man came into a tavern where I was trying to make a few dollars. Unfortunately—or fortunately, as it turned out—he refused to be hustled and persuaded me to try bartending at the restaurant he owned. I liked that because I'm a night person. From there I progressed into managing restaurants and eventually owning my own. It was a sort of snowball effect. Nothing to it."

She admired his candor, but realized at the same time that even her parents wouldn't have thought much of the background he'd just described. Nor would Craig or David. And *they* certainly wouldn't approve of her sitting here with this man, even if she had drunk only coffee. "I'd better be getting back to the bus," she said awkwardly, standing up.

"Some of the people might want to put packages inside."

"You're closing me out again," he said, getting up, also. His voice was regretful.

She looked at him, then wished she hadn't. He was unsettling to be with, this man. He had a way of making eye contact and holding it longer than was usual—or necessary. He was looking at her solemnly now, his dark eyes holding hers so that she couldn't possibly look away. Once again she was irresistibly reminded of a gambler. He had an air about him that said he always expected to win. She felt as though the floor of the *hostería* was gradually opening beneath her feet and she was falling, falling.

"You wouldn't really have held out on the children if I'd refused to sing, would you?" she asked.

He shook his head, smiling faintly. "I love children too much to treat them badly."

"I was conned."

He nodded. Then he looked solemn again. "I'd like to talk to you sometime soon," he said.

"Haven't we been talking?"

"I have a proposition for you." He grinned wickedly as she backed away a step. "A *business* proposition."

She looked at him skeptically, and he assumed an innocent expression. "Are you free this evening? Perhaps we could have dinner."

"I'm already...I have a date," she said firmly.

"Tomorrow, then? At Chez Michel? Shall we say, seven o'clock?"

The thought came to her mind that David and Craig planned to go fishing the following evening. A friend who owned a small boat had invited them all, but Blythe had declined. She felt like a traitor for even considering seeing Michael again. All the same, she was intensely curious.

"I don't think—" she began, but he waved her protest aside with one long-fingered hand and interrupted in an aggrieved tone. "Surely you can't imagine I'm trying to deceive you, Blythe. If I wanted to make an assignation with you, I'd come right out with it, you know that. This is strictly business, I assure you."

His expression was still serious, and she hesitated, wondering what on earth he could have in mind. "We could talk on the bus," she suggested.

He shook his head. "I don't discuss business deals in front of other people." He paused. "Believe me, Blythe, this is nothing you could possibly take exception to."

"I'll think about it," she said finally, conscious that the patrons of the *hostería* were all watching them curiously as they lingered inside the doorway.

He seemed satisfied by her answer—which was perhaps one of the reasons she started thinking she might safely meet with him. The other reasons included the sudden thought that he might want to make a deal wherein he would recommend Wanderlust Tours, while she in turn recommended his restaurants—which could work out well for both of them, and for Craig and David, too. Michael Channing's restaurants were among the most popular in town. That gave rise to the thought that as they *were* so popular, he hardly needed any recommendations—which made her start wondering again if he had something devious in mind.

All the way back to San Diego, she pondered his request, deciding first yes, then no. He didn't try to influence her at all. Mostly he talked with the

Schmidts, drawing them out in the charming way that seemed natural to him. The rest of the group were engrossed in their purchases. The Frenchman had bought an enormous turtle shell and was wondering how he'd get it on the airplane. The New Zealanders were exclaiming over the fact that they'd seen clothes designed by Givenchy and René and the Israeli Diva in a store in Tijuana, and the Oregon women were poring over bird books they'd bought. She had plenty of time to think. Yet she couldn't seem to make up her mind.

By the time she drove up in front of the Holiday Inn again, she'd just about decided to refuse Michael's invitation. So it surprised her when she found herself telling him yes.

He stood on the sidewalk, smiling down at her in a very self-satisfied way. Then he put both hands on her shoulders and very gently kissed her mouth, his lips lingering on hers for no more than a second. She heard herself give a barely perceptible sigh.

"You won't be sorry, Blythe," he said softly, but she already suspected that she would.

3

THE COFFEE WAS STRONG AND BLACK, served demitasse, a fitting finale to the wonderful meal of roast lamb with braised shallots and herb butter, accompanied by potatoes parisienne and steamed snow peas. Blythe couldn't remember when she'd enjoyed a meal so much. She had savored every mouthful. She had occasionally dined this way with Craig and David but only on special occasions such as birthdays, or the day they'd bought the second bus. All of their profits were plowed back into the company and there wasn't much left for luxuries. "That Caesar salad was out of this world," she said with an appreciative sigh.

Michael smiled. "We wilt the romaine with hot water, then chill it," he told her. "It crisps up more that way."

He gestured at the dessert cart that was loaded with pastries and gateaux as glossy and appetizing as the cover of *Gourmet* magazine, but she shook her head without looking at it. "Don't you dare tempt me," she said, laughing, then realized as Michael's eyebrows quirked that she'd committed another double entendre.

He didn't follow it up this time, and she decided she'd finally convinced him to drop his pursuit of her. He'd certainly been a perfect host so far. From the moment he'd picked her up at the apartment she shared with David, through the sampling, approving and ordering of the wine and the dinner itself, he had behaved with impeccable courtesy. He had not yet explained the business proposition he had in mind, murmuring, "Later," when Blythe attempted to bring it up.

"I suppose there really is a business proposition?" she'd said dryly, and he'd answered with a feigned expression of outraged innocence that had made her laugh, while at the same time making her wonder if she had been conned again. All the same, she had enjoyed herself. When she ate out with David and Craig *she* usually ordered the wine and they always split the check three ways, haggling good-humoredly over who had eaten the noodles, who the baked potato. But this had been a night out of the glamorous sort her parents had always enjoyed. The waiters had been especially attentive, treating Michael with a deference that bordered on reverence. The manager had come in to assure himself they were being treated properly. The waitresses had almost fallen over themselves with eagerness to serve him—which hadn't surprised her.

The restaurant was attractive. It had the fresh and airy ambience of a contemporary European café, complete with plants and tubs of bright flowers, crisp linen tablecloths and wall racks filled with imported wines. Added to this was a commanding view of the harbor.

Michael was wearing a dark suit with a decidedly British cut that complimented his lean body to perfection and was set off by a whiter-than-white shirt and a Hermès tie that wasn't quite as tightly knotted as it should be. His dark hair was obviously meticulously clean and recently trimmed but, as al-

ways, casually untidy, making him once again the
picture of careless elegance. Blythe had pulled out of
a cedar chest a Byzantine-patterned silk dress by
Jack Mulqueen that her mother had given her on her
twentieth birthday, knowing that its swirl of fall colors did wonders for her light-brown eyes and honey-
colored tresses. She had left her hair loose and waving
to her shoulders for the occasion, not because of Michael's announced preference but because the low
square neck of the dress demanded it. Together, she
thought, she and Michael looked like an illustration
from the pages of *Town and Country*.

As she sipped her coffee, she gradually became
aware that every head in the place was turning toward their table. "What are they looking at?" she
asked Michael nervously.

He leaned forward and smiled deeply, theatrically,
into her eyes. "Looking as beautiful as you do, how
can you ask?"

She let out her breath in exasperation. But before
she could reply, they were interrupted by a voice
saying, "Is this the chick?" and she turned, astonished, as a wiry Filipino with a mop of black ringlets
dropped an arm around her shoulders and grinned
at her with apparent approval. He was wearing a
white suit and a hot-pink shirt, open at the throat to
show a silver medallion. She recognized him at once.
Domingo. Now she understood the stares. Domingo
had recently begun to achieve fame locally. David
referred to him as one of the finest guitarists he'd
ever heard, the kind he couldn't hope to be himself.
Domingo and his group, Temptation, played three
nights a week in the Starlight Room at Chez Michel.
The *San Diego Union* had written him up a month or
so ago, calling the group "powerful, dynamic, a
must-see."

He spoke not to her but to Michael, as though she weren't there. "You were right, man. She's as decorative to the max as all the other beauties you've brought in here. You must have cornered the market in San Diego. The question, is, can this one sing?"

"She can sing," Michael said.

The young man walked around her and sat down on her other side, but he didn't relax. His fingers tapped rhythmically and constantly on the table and he held his body rigid, as though he were having to restrain it from moving to the hard-hitting beat of his own music. After a moment he leaned one elbow on the table and looked at her intently. "What kind of repertoire you got?"

She stared at him blankly, and he gave an impatient shrug. "We play everything from country ballads to rock and disco. Can you cut it?"

As she continued to look bewildered, he turned to Michael, who was laughing. "Take it easy, Dom," Michael said. "Blythe doesn't know yet that I asked you to come in to meet her."

Domingo glanced from Michael to Blythe then back again and seemed to reach some conclusion of his own. "Like that, is it?" he said, then patted Blythe's hand where it lay on the table. "Let's start over, babe. You're a singer right?"

She nodded.

"What kind of songs you sing?"

"Every kind," she faltered. "Rock, country, folk, blues."

"Now we're getting some kind of place. You're going to sing for me tonight like Mr. Channing arranged, right?"

"Wrong." She understood at last what was going on. And her first reaction was cold fury. How dared Michael Channing set this up without even consulting her! Was he trying to impress her with his power so she could be properly grateful? "This is the business proposition?" she asked Michael with frost in her voice.

He nodded, smiling with self-satisfaction, obviously expecting her to fall all over him with gratitude.

She looked levelly into the dancing black eyes of the other man. "Mr. Channing invited me to dinner to discuss business. Period."

"Man, you're devious," Domingo said over his shoulder, but his eyes didn't leave Blythe's. "Listen, babe, we're not suggesting cruel and unusual punishment here. You don't have to look at me like I spilled punch on the duchess's skirt. Mr. Channing's never tried to influence me before, so you must have something. And he's offering you what money can't buy—the chance to sing with the greatest."

"I hadn't realized you were so modest," Michael murmured.

Blythe couldn't prevent a spurt of laughter, and her anger dissolved as though it had never existed. At least it seemed that this kind of thing wasn't standard practice for Michael Channing. He evidently hadn't suggested any of the "other beauties" Domingo had mentioned should sing.

"Modesty doesn't get you anywhere in this trade," Domingo remarked. He straightened and stood up, looking down at her. "I guess I came on the scene ahead of schedule," he said. "But this is the deal. Mr. Channing wants me to hear you sing—I say okay. You want to play hard to get—that's okay, too. But you have to make up your mind now. We've got twenty minutes before you'll be auditioning in front of a live audience, so what do you say? You want to go for it?"

Excitement suddenly bubbled up inside Blythe. Perhaps it was the effect of the wine she'd drunk or the overpowering energy of this novel young man, but she felt all at once as Cinderella must have felt when she found out she really was going to the ball.

And like Cinderella, she seemed to be magically transported out of the room as soon as she nodded her head. Afterward she couldn't remember saying anything to Domingo at all. She just remembered Michael standing up, beaming like a magician who'd produced a dove when everyone expected a rabbit, or Ricardo Montalban orchestrating someone's fantasy. "I'll deal with you later," she threatened, then let herself be led by one hand toward the lounge.

She was stiff and anxious at first, but then Domingo's sheer skill with the guitar aroused her admiration and made her forget her own self-consciousness. She found herself tackling songs with more freedom than she ever had, letting her voice take over, instead of controlling it as she usually did. The other members of the group appeared and started filling in—Stacey Livingston, a slim black man who spent his time boxed in by an organ, a mini-Moog synthesizer and a Mellotron, a keyboard that could duplicate with fair fidelity the sound of a string section; and Eddie Francis, a good-looking towhead who played the drums. Gradually people started coming into the lounge.

It seemed to be taken for granted that she'd go on singing even after the room started filling up. Some of the songs she hadn't heard before. Domingo told her in the first break that the group played a lot of standards—"evergreens," he called them with a groan in his voice—but that they often sneaked in

some of their own material. Stacey informed her that
their former singer was having a baby and wanted
to try domesticity for a while. He complimented her
on her voice during that first break. So did Eddie, the
drummer. Domingo didn't say a word, and she
thought perhaps he'd tell her the "audition" was finally over. But after fifteen minutes he stood up and
tapped her on the shoulder and said, "Back to
work," and she found herself once again in front of
the microphone, marveling at the full rich sound of
her own voice as it came back to her through the
monitor after it had passed through the amplifiers.
The group had the best PA equipment she'd ever
heard.

She had never exercised her voice as much, hadn't
even realized she was capable of such diversity. The
well-dressed crowd in the Starlight Room seemed to
enjoy anything they could move to, and Temptation
provided a mixture of dance music, everything from
dreamy fox-trots to wild tunes with a touch of reggae. Her voice held out, mostly because she was affected by the unique talents of the other members of
the group, energized by their high level of performance.

The audience loved them—that was obvious. And
Blythe in turn loved the audience; loved the warmth
and approval she could feel coming from them as
she sang; loved the way each couple danced, each
with its own style. Middle-aged couples gyrated
in stately swing steps, while the younger patrons
flailed wildly and the more elderly danced a sort of
jigging two-step to whatever was played. There
were a lot of requests, mostly for Domingo's de-
spised "evergreens" but occasionally for one of the

songs the group had written. Blythe liked their lyrics, which dealt mostly with love, returned and unrequited, but without the moon-June flavor of the standards. These songs were as contemporary as Corvettes and jet skis, fast and furious in style. Not knowing the words, she harmonized while Domingo and Stacey sang. She felt she could go on all night.

After the second break, Domingo gave in to audience pressure and provided a demonstration of break dancing, becoming a whirling dervish of arms and legs, dancing on his hands, his back and even his head. Galvanized by the stunning performance, the audience crowded around the dance floor, clapping in time to the beat, cheering when Stacey took Domingo's place and performed just as incredibly. Teasing her when he was done, Stacey tilted his head to one side and grinned at her, his eyes indicating it was her turn. She nodded agreement, then parodied a demure waltz in place, which drew a roar of laughter from the audience. And then Domingo began the intro to a hard-rock song. The others filled in almost immediately and the small stage exploded with sound. Blythe didn't know the lyrics, so she stepped back and watched the dancers until the second number, "Heartbreaker," a Pat Benatar song that was one of her favorites.

The set was almost over when she noticed Michael. He was standing at the back of the room watching her, lean and dark, unsmiling, propped against the wall as though he'd been standing there for a long time. When he caught her gaze he smiled and gave her a little salute with two fingers. She felt a response that was so strong it was almost tangible.

Immediately she looked away and concentrated on her singing, conscious all the time that he was watching her.

Nobody left until the lounge closed at 1:00 A.M. Nobody ever left the Starlight until closing time, Domingo told her. In spite of the late hour, Blythe didn't feel tired. She felt as though she were flying, soaring upward toward some distant star. At the same time she was holding her breath—figuratively, at least—waiting for some comment from Domingo to let her know if he liked her singing or not. It shouldn't really be important to her, she told herself as she sat sipping decaffeinated coffee, watching the group checking on some minor flaw in the PA system that only Domingo had heard. The whole evening had been a time out of mind, a once-in-a-lifetime opportunity to translate fantasy into reality. Tomorrow she would come down to earth—in less than six hours, in fact. She was driving the city tour tomorrow, twice. But still, she was anxious to hear Domingo's opinion. She hadn't ever had a professional opinion—outside of school, which didn't really count.

Domingo was not one to beat around the bush. "A little sterile some of the time," he said when he joined her finally. "Could be a little gutsier. Not enough emotional impact. But different." He nodded, placed one foot on the chair next to her and leaned his elbow on one knee. "Different," he repeated, screwing up his eyes.

She felt a surge of disappointment that was out of all proportion. For a second she was tempted to hide herself under the table. "I'm grateful you gave me a chance to sing," she managed stiffly. "I enjoyed myself."

His black eyes narrowed on her face. "You should

wear more makeup, you know. Those lights...." He grinned over her head. "What you think, man?"

Michael's voice answered him. "I think I'd prefer to hear what you think."

Her heart started pounding. She wasn't sure if Michael's voice had caused the sudden increase in adrenaline, or the embarrassing prospect of his hearing Domingo's verdict.

"She needs more makeup," Domingo repeated. "And that dress is a disaster, man." He grinned at Blythe as she opened her mouth to defend her choice of costume. "I know, you thought you were just going out for dinner. And you look real—" he paused, looking up at the ceiling for inspiration "—classy," he concluded with a scowl. "Not an image that goes with Temptation. Are you punctual?"

She stared at him blankly. "She's a tour guide," Michael answered for her. "She has to be punctual."

Domingo had apparently reached some kind of decision. He nodded several times to himself, then said, "Rehearsal, seven tomorrow. Okay?"

"You're offering me a singing job?" Amazement made her voice squeak.

"No, I want you to scrub the stage," he replied. "Of course I'm talking about singing. Couple of weeks trial, find out how the audience reacts. Then we see. Three weekends, Friday, Saturday, Sunday. Two-hour rehearsal before, one or two hours the rest of the week. We have to teach you how to move. What you think?"

"But I thought you didn't like my voice...." Blythe's words trailed off as Domingo looked at her with apparent exasperation.

"You want praise? I already told you you got something different. What you think matters in this business? Sure, you got a little bit Sheena Easton, a little bit Pat Benatar, but the rest sounds like no one I ever heard. You got a good sound. An honest sound. Good range. Need to round out on the high notes, maybe. What makes you think I don't like your voice? I'm a professional, right? You didn't have a voice you wouldn't have lasted ten minutes tonight. What more you want me to say?"

"I think he likes you," Michael said dryly. "I've never heard him explain himself before."

"*I* think she's dynamite," Stacey said as he passed by carrying one of Domingo's guitars.

"Like I said," Domingo put in.

Elation was replacing disappointment and embarrassment. "You really think I can sing?"

Domingo looked over her head at Michael again. "I can't make this chick out. What she think I've been talking about?" He looked at Blythe. "You want the job or not?"

"I want it, I'd love it, but...." Sanity was beginning to prevail. "I have a business, responsibilities. I can't possibly...."

Domingo straightened and started to walk away. "You make up your mind by tomorrow," he threw over his shoulder. Then he turned around. "You got the kind of voice the microphone loves," he said magnanimously. "All I got to do is teach you how to use it." He paused. "You decide to turn up, wear a jump suit. This color." He touched the collar of his hot-pink shirt. "And more makeup," he added as he went out.

Michael turned the chair next to Blythe around and straddled it, leaning on the back of it, smiling. "Do I have a new employee?" he asked.

Blythe stared at him, feeling very much as though

she'd been hit over the head with a two-by-four.
Which was hardly surprising. After a full day's
work she'd sung for close to four hours, give or take
a break or two. Her earlier high had dissipated suddenly, leaving her exhausted. And she had to be up
by seven—no, six. After the heat of the stage lights
and the energy she'd put into her singing, she'd
have to wash her hair. "It's impossible, Michael. I
have to do two tours tomorrow and again Sunday.
Weekends are our busiest times."

"You could try it for a couple of weeks."

"No, I can't. Craig would—"

"He wouldn't approve?"

"Well, of course he'll be delighted I've been offered such a chance," Blythe said slowly. "But he'll
realize, as I do, that the pressure would be tremendous, not to mention the lack of sleep."

"What time does your tour get in tomorrow?"

"Four-thirty, but that's not the point. I have
paperwork to do, housework, cooking. We all take
our share."

He was looking at her levelly. "I think I'll call you
Daisy," he said abruptly.

Blythe blinked. "'Daisy'?" she echoed blankly.

"When I was a kid I had a gerbil named Daisy."
He smiled reminiscently. "Odd creatures, gerbils.
Daisy led a very satisfactory life for a gerbil. She had
a wheel to run around in, good food, even an occasional lettuce leaf. I guess she was happy in her cage,
because whenever I encouraged her to come out of it
she'd huddle back in a corner and twitch her whis-
kers. Her whole body would tremble until I closed
the door."

Blythe's mouth had been slowly tightening
throughout this recital. "An interesting analogy, Mr.

Channing," she said when his dark glance challenged her. "But I'm hardly in a cage."

"Aren't you?"

She stood up. "I have to go, I'm afraid." She forced herself to meet his gaze, which was as she remembered it once before, filled with understanding. Which was pretty patronizing of him. "I appreciate your letting me sing in your nightclub," she said stiffly. "I really did enjoy myself, but I can't possibly take Domingo up on his offer, flattering as it is."

He hadn't moved. He was staring at the stage as though she were still performing there, his eyes thoughtful. "I'm remembering your face in that *hostería* in Tijuana," he said slowly. "When I asked if you'd ever thought of singing professionally, you looked so wistful for a few minutes. Like a little girl looking through a gap in a wall at the most beautiful garden she'd ever seen. Your eyes were extraordinary in that moment...golden."

"Having a fantasy is one thing. Acting it out isn't always wise."

"Why not?"

"I have to earn my living, Michael."

"You'll get $150 a night, same as the last singer."

"What was she like?" Blythe asked, suddenly curious.

Michael shrugged. "Young, dark haired, all leg warmers and lip gloss. A bit shrill for my taste."

One hundred fifty dollars. That was four hundred fifty a week, thirteen hundred fifty altogether. They could use the money. But still....

She shook her head. "I don't know, Michael."

She thought he'd seize on the sudden doubt in her voice, but instead he stood up, his expression unreadable. "Come on, I'll take you home."

In the parked car she looked at his averted profile. Was he angry with her, angry that she'd thrown his gift to her back in his face? "I'm sorry, Michael, really. I'd love to do it, but I have to be realistic."

He nodded. He still hadn't started the car or even turned on the lights. He was sitting very still, gazing through the windshield at the quarter moon that hung directly above the parking lot like a slice of honeydew melon. After a few minutes of silence, she saw the white flash of his smile in the darkened glass. "Still hiding, aren't you, Daisy?" he teased, and she realized he hadn't been fuming as she'd thought, but plotting his next attack.

"I'm not afraid," she insisted.

He turned to look at her directly. In the dim light of the parking area she could see the disbelieving slant of his eyebrows. "I'm not stupid," she said hotly. "I realize fabulous opportunities like this don't come along every day. Domingo is fantastic...my brother's convinced he'll be nationally known pretty soon. And having met him, heard him, I'm sure he wouldn't invite me to sing with the group unless he thought I had possibilities, potential—"

"Do you hear yourself, Blythe? Do you hear what you're saying? 'Fabulous,' 'fantastic.'" Michael had gripped her shoulders as he spoke and was shaking her lightly. "You loved it up there. You came alive. I *saw* you. And you know damn well you could do it, at least for a couple of weeks. You can catch up on your sleep later. You're not sixty years old, Blythe. You can take a chance. Just once in your life, don't be afraid to take a chance. *You* could be great, too. I thought that when I heard you at the wedding, but I was afraid the sentiment of the occasion might be clouding my judgment. Then, when I listened to you in Tijuana, I knew you could be special. You heard Domingo. You've got the kind of voice a microphone loves. You think he said that lightly?"

"I've taken lots of chances," she protested, trying to ignore the excitement that had filled her the moment he touched her.

"Name one."

"The business—going into business."

"Backed by your brother and what's his name. What kind of risk was that? This is *your* chance, Blythe. *Yours alone.* Don't turn your back on it."

She looked at him wonderingly, amazed by the intensity of his voice. "Why does it matter so much to you?" she asked.

His breath exploded. "Dammit, woman, I can't stand it when someone doesn't live up to his or her full potential. It's such a waste of—" He broke off and tugged at her shoulders. "Words aren't working," he muttered. "We have to try something else."

She thought he was going to shake her again and braced herself to resist, but instead he leaned toward her, and then his mouth came down on hers hard, stealing her breath. His lips moved over hers as though he could force a response from her by insisting, demanding....

And she *was* responding. The taste of his mouth was triggering something strange and frightening inside her, something that was just as demanding as his mouth, but more potent, because it came from a need of her own. She reached to hold him close, her hands stroking the back of his neck, gentling him. And now *he* responded. His body stilled and his mouth softened, brushing hers with infinite delicacy. His tongue lightly traced the inner contours of her mouth, finding her own tongue, flirting play-fully, drawing it gently into his own mouth. His hands slid down from her shoulders, barely grazing the thin silk of her dress, spreading sweet chaos in their wake, pulling her closer until she was pressed tightly against him.

Behind her closed eyelids, lights exploded gently in cascades of color like slowly falling stars. Some-where low in her body a pulse started beating, a pulse she hadn't known existed. Her blood had been replaced by a wild, honeyed sweetness that flowed through every part of her, a sweetness that began and ended in Michael's mouth. In his arms all of her senses seemed to come together in concentric circles, spinning and whirling. Her hearing picked up the sound of her own heartbeat and Michael's, both er-ratic; her sense of smell recorded salt air through the open car window, plus the smell of Michael, clean, masculine. Touch was there, too, with his hands burning through the silk of her dress and the slight erotic rasp of his cheek on her chin as his mouth moved down to her throat and pressed against the pulse that was beating just as erratically there.

Then he was kissing her mouth again, and her sight returned to the dark of her mind to marvel at the lights moving closer together, forming a perfect tiny circle like a degree sign, fading to a pinpoint of light, flaring out again.

Afterward she had no way to gauge how long their kiss had lasted. A minute, two, infinity. Nor could she remember who ended it. She remembered only the caressing sound of Michael's voice mur-muring, "Blythe, darling," and feeling that she wanted to cry with gladness at the tenderness in it.

A long time later, it seemed, he lifted his head and looked at her. He wasn't smiling, but his eyes were ebony bright. "I take it all back," he said softly. "You aren't going to be special. You are special."

"You, too," she whispered.

His lips brushed hers lightly once more. Then with the low sigh of a man awakening from a dream, he said, "I suppose I'd better get you home, or you won't have enough energy to sing tomorrow." There was a definite note of mischief in his voice now.

She laughed. "You're incorrigible."

"I know. But you are going to do it, aren't you?"

Somewhere during that wonderful kiss she had misplaced all the sensible reasons for turning down Domingo's offer. "I'm going to think about it," she told him.

IT WAS PAST TWO IN THE MORNING, and the apartment was dark. Carefully Blythe removed her key from the lock and closed the door slowly, hoping to avoid waking David. But to her dismay, as the door clicked shut, a light flashed on in his bedroom and she heard his voice say, "There she is."

In the next moment, not only David but Craig emerged from David's bedroom. Both were in pajamas and robes. David looked bleary eyed, and Craig's light-brown hair was unusually untidy. They'd evidently gone to sleep, but had programmed themselves to wake up at the slightest sound. "Where the hell have you been?" Craig demanded.

Guiltily conscious that her face might *show* what she'd been doing—it felt . . . glowing, as though she'd spent the day lying out in the sun—Blythe tried to sound casual as she reached down to turn on a lamp beside the sofa. "What on earth are you both doing up at this hour? Seems to me we have a busy day tomorrow."

"We got to bed at ten," David said virtuously, tightening the sash of his white terry robe around his rangy body.

Craig was wearing one of David's other robes, a gray velour that matched the stormy light in his eyes. "You didn't answer my question," he said.

"Because you won't believe the answer," Blythe said lightly. She turned to David, mostly to avoid the accusing look in Craig's eyes. "You'll never guess, Dave. You know Domingo, the guitarist? He's asked me to sing with him and his group. For a couple of weeks. In the Starlight Room. That's what I've been doing tonight, singing."

Pirouetting around the room as elation surged up in her again, she stopped at the old upright piano, lifted the lid and hammered out some triumphant-sounding chords, then whirled to face Craig. "Domingo liked my voice, Craig. Can you imagine? He said the microphone loved me."

Craig's eyes showed bewildered shock, but the accusation had disappeared. Encouraged, she flung herself down on the sofa and smiled up at the two men. "What do you think?" she asked.

"Hey, all right," David exclaimed. "Domingo. Wow! Congratulations." He sat down next to her and hugged her. "How did this all come about? How did you get to meet Domingo? You really sang tonight? In front of an audience? What did you sing?"

"Everything." She laughed. "Well, not quite everything. The group has a lot of stuff I don't know, but Domingo's offered to rehearse me."

Conscious of Craig's silence, she glanced up at him. Her breath caught in her throat. He looked... stunned, and curiously defenseless with his brown hair tumbling over his forehead like a little boy's. "If I decide to take him up on the offer, I'm going to have to work very hard," she said hastily. "I have to learn a lot in a short time. But it's a tremendous opportunity. I'd be singing three nights a week, Fridays, Saturdays and Sundays, but it's only a two-week trial and I could take the shorter tours those days, couldn't I? And fit the rehearsals in. If I decide to go ahead, that is."

She was going on too long, telling too much, throwing it all at him without giving herself a chance to see how he was taking it. "You wouldn't have to worry about the bookkeeping," she added with a nervous laugh. "I'm sure I could keep up with it."

Craig sat down heavily on the arm of the sofa and touched her cheek with one hand. "You really want this, don't you?" he said wonderingly.

"I'm tempted," she admitted.

One corner of his mouth twitched a little, but in a grimace, not a smile. "Does Michael Channing have anything to do with this fabulous offer?"

She flinched inwardly and at once felt tremendously guilty. "He arranged the audition, yes," she said carefully. "Wasn't that kind of him? He heard me sing at the wedding, remember, and he thought Domingo might like my voice."

She could hear the false note in her words. She was trying too hard to make the whole thing sound innocent, as though there had been no rush of passion between the two of them, no kisses that tasted of intimacies yet to come.

She glanced back at David, afraid the memory of those kisses might be showing on her face. "I guess we ought to get to bed. We're all going to be dead tomorrow."

David stood up promptly. "I'm off, anyway," he said. "Fishing wore us out, so Craig stopped over. You might have left a note," he added mildly.

"I thought I was just going to . . . ." No, it was probably best not to say Michael had inveigled her with talk of a business proposition. "I thought it would be better to see how I did before saying anything," she amended. "I might have bombed, you know."

"Not my sister." He reached down and ruffled her hair. "You look very pretty, by the way. I haven't seen you in that dress for a long time."

"Domingo didn't think much of it," Blythe admitted. "I'm supposed to wear a hot-pink jump suit if I take the job. Can you see me in hot pink?"

He tilted his head, considering. "It will match your cheeks," he said. "I don't know when I've seen you look so . . . lively."

She felt her cheeks flush even hotter. "I've always enjoyed singing, Dave," she said slowly. "You know that."

His light eyebrows rose. "Did I criticize? I'm all for it if that's what you really want. And I'm glad Domingo recognizes talent when he hears it." He leaned down and kissed her on the forehead. "However, I'm pooped." He crossed the small living room to his bedroom and glanced back. "Don't worry about the schedule," he added. "We can work it out."

Silence descended. Blythe glanced around the living room, taking comfort in its familiarity, its cheerful simplicity. She and David had managed to save some of the less expensive pieces of furniture from the auction that had disposed of their old sumptuous house. With the addition of lots of pillows and several plants they'd made the boxlike apartment into a home.

She was afraid to look at Craig. Of all the nights for him to stay over. He often did, but tonight of all nights.... "Did you catch any fish?" she asked at last.

"No." Silence. "The water was a bit rough. We didn't stay out long."

"I'm sorry I wasn't here," she murmured when the silence became uncomfortable again.

"That's okay. We were just worried when it got so late. It's not like you."

"Maybe I'm too predictable," she said, trying to lighten the atmosphere.

He laughed softly, and she felt relieved. "I like you predictable," he said firmly.

"But you wouldn't be mad if I accepted Domingo's offer?"

"Of course not. What kind of creep do you think I am? I've always loved your voice. How could I object to anyone else loving it?"

The words were fine, but there was a stiltedness to his voice that worried her. Or was she reading her own doubt into his voice? Why did she suddenly wish he'd say something definite, one way or the other? If he was to forbid her to take the job she'd have something solid to fight about. But that was stupid. Craig wouldn't dream of forbidding her to do anything. He didn't have that much claim on her. Perhaps that was part of the trouble. "Craig," she said tentatively, looking up at him.

He slid down beside her, moving her over on the sofa, and put an arm around her shoulders. "Don't be an idiot. Of course I wouldn't mind. And I'm as delighted as Dave that you did so well. Tomorrow I'll be as enthusiastic as can be. I'm just tired. And I was disappointed that you weren't here. I'd hoped . . . well, it's been a while since we spent any time alone together."

She leaned her head against his shoulder, trying to suppress the sudden flash of resentment she felt. Was he deliberately trying to make her feel guilty? Or was the guilt coming from inside her?

"You think it's frivolous, don't you?" Blythe asked after another awkward pause.

Craig shrugged. "Singing? I suppose I do."

"I will get paid, you know." She attempted a laugh. "We could use the money."

"You'd be doing it for the money?" His voice was dry, disbelieving.

"Why else?" she asked tightly.

"Well, you do tend to be insecure. Maybe you're just looking for some attention? You know, your parents were always—"

"Don't you criticize my parents, Craig Foster," she snapped, turning to glare at him.

He looked at her with surprise. "Why not? You and David do it all the time."

"We do it with love," she said hotly. "I know mom and dad were . . . irresponsible, but we loved them. And in any case, this has nothing to do with them. This is something *I* want to do."

"I thought you wanted the business as much as I did," he said in a voice that was suddenly doleful. He had removed his arm from behind her. He was leaning forward now, looking down at his hands, clasped between his knees. His profile was in shadow, but she could see he was genuinely upset.

She felt a tug at her heart and forced herself to speak more calmly. "Of course I want the business. I wouldn't neglect it just because I was singing. I wouldn't even think of doing it if I thought it would seriously disrupt our schedule, believe me."

"What about us? When would I be able to see you?"

"I'd have *some* free time. I know it wouldn't be much, but it would only be for a couple of weeks, Craig."

"Promise?"

"Promise what?"

His mouth had set in a straight line. "You said this would be a trial. What if Domingo wants you to stay on? I want you to promise me you won't do it for more than two weeks. Then it's okay. I guess."

"It's hardly likely I'll be offered a permanent job," Blythe protested, realizing at the same time that it could happen. If she was good enough. She felt a sudden return of the soaring sensation she'd experienced earlier and knew with a rush of excitement that she was going to accept Domingo's offer.

"I'm not going to make any promises," she said firmly, suddenly feeling terribly disappointed in Craig. If he really cared for her, he should be happy she'd been offered this opportunity. And no matter what he said, she could tell he was dismayed. He hadn't even congratulated her. "I'm sorry you don't approve, Craig, but I am going to sing at the Starlight Room. I've decided. After the trial period, if Domingo does want me to stay on, then I'll have another decision to make, but I'm not going to—"

"Hey, listen, what are we fighting about?" Craig said suddenly, affectionately. "I told you I don't mind for a couple of weeks, and probably that will be the end of it, anyway."

Another flash of resentment shot through Blythe. Did he have so little faith in her chances?

Apparently aware he'd annoyed her again, Craig put his arm around her, smiling in his usual loving manner. His gray eyes narrowed seductively, crinkling at the corners in the way she usually loved, but that didn't move her at all tonight. "What do you say we kiss and make up?"

She shook her head. "I'm not exactly in a loving mood right now."

His smile faded. Then he said in a hesitant way that was unlike him, "I'm sorry, honey." He looked directly into her eyes, his face solemn. "I have a confession to make. I guess I'm jealous about Michael Channing's part in this. Even if I don't like the guy, I can see he has a lot more to offer a woman than I do...money and the kind of life you used to have...." His voice trailed away. "If we were better fixed and could get married, instead of waiting until the business is safely established...."

She felt a melting sensation inside. This was the first time he'd referred to marriage in a serious way. And he looked so suddenly unsure of himself, not at all like the usual confident Craig. There was guilt in her, too. If he knew she'd let Michael kiss her.... No, that wasn't strictly true. She hadn't just *accepted* Michael's kiss; she had responded to it totally. She could still recall that languorous sweetness that had invaded her when.... "I probably won't even see Michael Channing again," she said abruptly. "He does have other restaurants, after all." She put one

hand on Craig's arm, felt how tense it was and softened again. "I thought you'd be pleased for me," she
said quietly, almost pleadingly.

He relaxed at once, smiling. "I am pleased," he
said. "And we won't fight anymore. I've been acting
like a jealous idiot. I can see that. Of course I'm
pleased for you. And you have my permission to go
right ahead and sing your little heart out." He
leaned over and kissed her cheek. "As long as you
remember who your heart belongs to."

About to point out that she hadn't asked his permission, didn't have to ask his permission and that
he hadn't ever really staked a claim on her heart, she
swallowed her indignation and nodded apparent
agreement.

His arm tightened around her, urging her toward
him. Probably he wanted to kiss her. How could she
kiss him after kissing Michael? And enjoying it so
thoroughly.

She stood up quickly. "I'm exhausted," she said
truthfully.

"Of course you are." There was only warm understanding in his voice now, which made her feel
even guiltier.

Standing, he put his arms lightly around her and
kissed the top of her head as though she were a little
girl, a cherished little sister. At any other time she
would have lifted her face for his kiss. He was after
all the first man she'd ever loved, the only man she'd
ever loved. But she sensed that if she did offer her
mouth for a kiss, he would want to go further. Even
now she could feel his arms tightening around her,
hear the quickening of his breath. "We decided," she
began, and heard him sigh.

"I know," he said.

Whenever they had wanted to make love they had always gone to Craig's apartment. Neither of them felt comfortable with the idea of intimacy when David was in another room. "The walls in this place are about as thick as Kleenex," David had often commented.

"We could go to my place," Craig murmured.

"It's much too late." She could feel her body stiffening. She had never been a promiscuous woman. She couldn't go straight from Michael's arms to Craig's. What she'd really wanted to do, when she came home, was to go quietly to her room, where she could lie in the dark and think about what had happened with Michael, try to make some sense out of her emotions, which were minute by minute becoming more and more confused.

"I know," Craig repeated. He set her at arm's length and smiled ruefully, looking so handsome, so dear, she felt all at once very loving toward him. Her feelings must have shown on her face. He grinned more naturally. "Tomorrow, maybe," he murmured.

"I'll be very late again, I'm afraid."

"Oh, yes, I'd forgotten."

He hadn't forgotten. How could he forget? *Was* he angry about her singing? For another second she looked at him, confused. Then she sighed. "I'm about to go to sleep on my feet," she said. "And I still have to wash my face."

He nodded, smiling again, releasing her. "I'll see you in the morning. I might even cook breakfast. Pancakes with blueberries. How does that sound?"

"Wonderful." She made herself smile, though her face felt as if it might crack, and then she turned toward her bedroom, feeling her shoulders slump with relief that Craig had at least come around.

Though they occasionally argued, they didn't usually fight. Blythe felt uncomfortable with anger.
She'd never really learned how to express it. Her
parents had always wanted her to be happy, so she'd
lived up to their expectations and buried any problems she might have.

Probably all that was wrong with Craig was the
prospect of a change in their well-ordered life. He
tended to enjoy the status quo, especially when
things were going well. She really did love him, she
thought as she slid into bed a few minutes later. He
was a very important part of her life—past, present
and future. As important as David, in a different
way.

So what was it she felt for Michael Channing?

She tried to build his face in her mind but came up
with only an assortment of planes and angles, intense dark eyes, a shock of black hair. Just when she
thought she had his image pinned down, it slipped
away from her like mercury.

Why mercury, she wondered, and her brain oblig-
ingly produced a memory. Once when she was a
child, running a fever, her mother had taken her temperature and then shaken the thermometer down too
hard, letting it slip from her fingers. Between them
they'd picked up every shard of glass, but they hadn't
been able to find the mercury, never had found it. Its
total disappearance had mystified Blythe for weeks.
Quicksilver, she thought, remembering the other
name for the heavy silver liquid.

She thought she might lie awake for hours, in
spite of her weariness. Her mind seemed wired, and
she ought really to try to sort through her jumbled
emotions, face up to the new feelings that were
plaguing her heart.

But when she woke in the morning she realized she hadn't lain awake at all; she'd slid immediately into a deep and apparently dreamless sleep.

THE PACKAGE WAS DELIVERED to the tour office by special messenger shortly after noon. David handed it to Blythe when she stopped off at the office between city tours. It was a white dress box, stuffed with tissue paper that was wrapped around a polished-cotton jump suit in a lush shade of hot pink.

Blythe shook out the suit and held it against her, looking at herself in the office mirror. The color did surprising things for her complexion, giving it a deep healthy glow, and her hair seemed brighter, glossier.

"Sexy," David commented from behind her.

She was suddenly glad that Craig had taken the La Jolla run and wouldn't be back for a couple of hours. She felt sure he wouldn't approve of the jump suit's plunging collar or its body-hugging lines.

"Domingo didn't say he'd provide the jump suit," she said, turning this way and that, wishing she had time to try it on. She glanced at the size tag. How had Domingo known she wore a size eight? A second later she noticed a card pinned to the sash. "Thought you might not have time for shopping. Love, Craig."

"Is anything wrong?" David asked.

She shook her head, though she felt like crying. After all her resentment, all the criticism she'd directed at Craig in her mind, he'd come up with the perfect way to show she had his blessing after all. After the way she'd treated him, lied by omission to him. After she'd let herself be tempted into Michael Channing's arms.

When she turned around, David had an odd expression on his face. Concern? "Are you sure nothing's wrong?"

She shook her head, almost unable to speak. "Craig sent it," she managed at last.

David grinned. "Isn't he the romantic? Next thing you know it'll be red roses." He laughed out loud, looking at her face. "What on earth are you looking so miserable about?" His expression changed abruptly. "You're not having second thoughts, are you, about singing? Don't tell me you're scared?"

She shook her head again. There was no way she could tell him it wasn't the singing she was afraid of but Michael Channing. There was no doubt in her mind that he was a threat to her neatly planned life. How long would Craig go on being such a good sport if Michael kept on....

David stood up and came around the desk and put his hands on her shoulders, smiling down at her, his golden-brown eyes fond. "Come on now, sis, I know when something's wrong with you, just as you know the same about me. We're eggs from the same basket, remember?"

It was an old joke between them, one started by their father, who had called her "Humpty" and him "Dumpty" when they were chubby toddlers. The memory made her smile, and she realized she was panicking over nothing. She was a strong woman; she'd made herself strong. It didn't matter that Michael Channing attracted her. She wasn't Red Riding Hood threatened by the big bad wolf. She was

Blythe Sherwood, captain of her own destiny. And if that wasn't mixing metaphors, she didn't know what was.

"That's better," David said as she laughed at herself. He hugged her briskly, then returned to the desk. "All the same," he added, looking up and catching her fond gaze with his. "If anything is bothering you, better you spit it out."

"Everything's fine," she assured him, convinced now that it would be.

LESS THAN AN HOUR into rehearsal that evening, Blythe discovered that Domingo was a perfectionist. He tested and retested the amplification and lights, seeming to have a complete grasp of the sophisticated electronics involved, swearing absentmindedly over the equipment in colorful bursts of language that Stacey told her was Tagalog. "Though you probably won't find those words in any Filipino dictionary," he added.

Once everything was set up to Domingo's satisfaction, he concentrated on Blythe.

She had a good honest sound, he told her again, but she had to learn to project the emotion and the mood of a song, to get down inside herself and come up with something more primitive, hard-hitting. And she had to learn to move.

"You have to lean on the music, let it get inside you, let it make love to you," he said.

It seemed fitting that Michael Channing chose that moment to come into the lounge. He waved at her, nodded to Domingo, Stacey and Eddie, then sat down at one of the little tables and ordered a glass of wine.

Blythe forced herself to concentrate on Domingo,

though every pore in her body was aware of the rakishly lean, impeccably suited man at the rear of the room.

After going through a few standards, Domingo had given her the lyrics to several of the group's own songs and was "talking" her through the first one, stressing the proper words, indicating the beat by slapping his guitar. "Like this, babe. 'I saw him, boom-boom, *walk*ing.'"

"Got it?" he asked after she'd chanted it through under her breath.

She nodded uncertainly, and he said, "Great. Let's get it on," and before she could feel self-conscious, she was singing the way he'd shown her, feeling suddenly shivery as she felt the music entering into her bones, carrying her along on its own waves of sound.

Michael applauded at the end, and Domingo glared at him. "You can't be quiet, man, you don't stay."

Michael mimed apology and promises of good behavior, and Domingo relented and murmured, "He's okay, that guy," to Blythe. And then blasted her for forgetting to move while she was singing. "You don't have to jive it up," he explained. "Just let your body relax, change weight on your feet, something."

"I'll try," she promised, and they were off again, this time into "For Your Eyes Only," a wonderfully moody song, but also one of the most difficult Blythe had ever sung.

This time Domingo found fault with Stacey. "The harmonies aren't sharp enough. We're getting a fuzzy sound in there somewhere." He waved Blythe off for a short break, and he and Stacey put their heads together over the synthesizer.

She couldn't really do anything else but walk over to Michael's table. He pulled out a chair for her, smiling sympathetically as she sank into it and reached for a paper napkin to mop her forehead. "Sorry you decided to take the job?" he asked.

"The man's a Tartar," she said, laughing. She shook her head. "No, I'm not sorry. Domingo's a superb musician. He catches the slightest fault in intonation or timing, and he won't let it go until he's satisfied we're all meshing smoothly. I've learned more in the past hour and a half than I did in two years of music composition and theory in college."

"I heard him complaining that you need to get in touch with your own emotions," he said, raising those impossibly slanted eyebrows of his. Such dark eyebrows. The same raven color as his hair. He really had the most wonderful hair, so thick and clean looking—usually slightly untidy, as though he made a habit of running his fingers through it. She found herself wondering how it would feel to run *her* fingers through it.

His dark gaze was on her mouth now, and she hurried into speech. "Craig bought me a jump suit," she told him. "I didn't change into it yet." That was pretty stupid. She was quite obviously wearing a T-shirt and blue jeans like the other members of the group. "I figured I'd get pretty hot during rehearsal," she added lamely.

His eyes and mouth showed amusement, and she knew he was thinking that she'd brought up Craig's name to protect herself. As though she needed an amulet to ward off the effects of his sensually suggestive eyes. She sighed. She really had to stop thinking she could read his mind.

"Do you remember our castle?" he asked with a lazy smile.

She looked at him blankly.

His expression became grave. "You've forgotten," he said with a hint of indignation. "I'm talking about the castle in Camelot where we planned to dance the night away."

The fantasy he'd spun for her when they danced at Julie's wedding. She *had* forgotten, had forced herself to forget. Why had he reminded her? She could suddenly feel again the closeness of his strong, lean body when they danced that day, the touch of his lips on her hand, the strange sensation that reality had ceased to exist around them.

For a few long moments she stared at him, caught up in the memory of that dance. Then she said tersely, "The existence of Camelot has never been historically proved. Most historians don't acknowledge the existence of King Arthur, either." She paused. "There might have been a general of the armies named Arthur," she conceded. "But by all accounts he was no more moral than the rest of the knights."

"Ouch," he said, wincing.

She gave him a smug smile. "David's a history major. I read a lot of his books when we were at school together."

"Didn't you ever read fantasy?"

"I didn't need to. My parents lived it. I found out it wasn't very practical."

"And you admire practicality?"

"I do."

His mouth turned down in a comical grimace. "I'm not making much headway here." Before she could reply, he became abruptly solemn.

"I've thought a lot about last night, Blythe," he

said softly. "I have an idea it was special to you. Am
I right?"

"I was...yes, it was special," she said honestly. "I
meant to talk to you about that. I wasn't really fair to
you. I guess I must still have been high on singing,
all the unexpectedness of the whole evening."

She couldn't go on looking at him, not when his
dark eyes held such loving amusement that her body
was starting to come alive with stirrings and mur-
murs of pleasure.

Somehow she managed to avert her gaze. "May I
have a glass of water, please," she called to the
young woman who was arranging bottles behind
the bar. Not waiting for an answer, she jumped up
and went to the bar to get it herself, then carried it
back with her gaze fixed on it, as though she'd spill
it if she didn't concentrate.

"You're saying that last night was an isolated
event?" Michael asked. "You were affected by the
evening, the moon, something outside yourself? The
feelings didn't come from inside? You don't want to
repeat the experience?"

Blythe took a deep swallow of water. His voice
was low, and he was weaving a spell around her
again, trying to get her to admit....

"I'm practically engaged to Craig Foster," she reminded him.

He didn't answer, and she was forced to look at
him. He was smiling wickedly. "*Practically* sounds
more promising than *unofficially.*"

She'd forgotten what she'd told him before. "I
probably am going to marry Craig someday," she
said weakly. "So there can't be any repetition of—"

"Why not?" he asked mildly.

Speechless, she gazed at him helplessly. He was

smiling blandly now, not giving any of his thoughts away. "You're not married yet—or even engaged. And I'm certainly not asking you to marry me. What I have in mind is a, shall we say, temporary arrangement." He lifted his eyebrows at her. "Surely you aren't the kind of young woman who expects a marriage proposal to be the logical outcome of every relationship? I had you pegged as much too level-headed for that."

She felt... what? Insulted? Disappointed? Angry? All of the above. She considered turning the tiny table over into his lap, wine, water and all. But before she could take any action, he sighed deeply.

"Some kind soul has probably told you that I'm divorced. As you might also have heard, the divorce was very painful. Even though it's ancient history now, it's not the sort of experience that encourages anyone to begin another serious relationship." He gave a mock shudder, then grinned. "Anyway, your Mr. Foster, though I'm sure he's a very worthwhile person, is not for you. You need someone who can plumb your depths. Someone like me," he added with such engaging false modesty that she was tempted to laugh—a temptation she resisted.

She managed to find her voice at last. "I've heard you change women every week," she said dryly, proud of her fast recovery. "I understand they're usually older women."

He nodded, looking suddenly bleak. "Older women are more... responsible."

"Why, me then?"

The bleak expression left his face, but she filed it away in her memory as something to ponder. "I have an idea you are a fairly responsible person," he said with a faint smile.

"Knowing me so well," she said curtly, "do you really think I'd be interested in a short-term fling?"

His smile widened. "I don't see why not. It would be very good for you."

While she stared at him, unable to decide if she should slap his face or heave a sigh of relief because she didn't have to worry about him after all, he reached one hand across the table and covered hers where it clasped the glass. At once she felt a shock of sexual awareness, which infuriated her.

Luckily Domingo called to her before she could tell Michael what she thought of his shoddy tricks, of his leading her on by talking of that fantasy he'd invented, letting her tell him last night had meant something to her, then informing her she'd overestimated his interest. There was a word for a man like that, she thought furiously as she hurried across the lounge to the stage. If she weren't a lady she'd turn around right now and use it to his face.

She thought he would probably leave right away, but he stayed for another half-hour, and he was there later that evening, standing at the back of the room again, watching her. She found herself singing as though her life depended on it, using the turbulent emotions he'd aroused in her to put the songs across in a way that soon had Domingo nodding at her with approval over the top of his guitar. He'd already told her she looked great in the jump suit, and the garment seemed to give her more freedom to move, which pleased him, also. She'd also experimented with makeup, using a dark-plum eyeshadow, more mascara and two shades of blusher to emphasize her cheekbones. Domingo approved her "new look" totally, telling her he'd been afraid the night before that she'd disappear under the bright stage lights. She found herself wondering now if Michael approved of the way she looked tonight. He certainly wasn't showing any disapproval as he watched her. Probably he was deciding how best he could insult her next.

She learned that night to draw on her own emotions, to feel a song instead of acting it. She thought of Craig telling her to "sing her little heart out," and that gave her the anger to do so. She watched Michael watching her and put a world of sarcasm and wounded feelings into "You're So Vain."

At first hoping he would go away, she began to be pleased he was there. His presence helped to keep her anger sharp, and that in itself would surely improve her performance.

At closing time, Domingo told her he was pleased with her, but she had to watch out not to overemote. "You got carried away there toward the last," he said.

"But you told me to project more emotion," she snapped, exasperated.

Domingo ran one hand through his black ringlets and cast a dramatically appealing glance at Stacey. "Isn't that just like a chick? Two nights of being a star and she's already got temperament!" But then he laughed and hugged her and explained that she had to include some positive emotion along with the negative, and not to forget the mood of the song. "You belted out 'Love Me Tender' like it was the theme from *Star Wars*," he exaggerated, which made her laugh and feel much better.

"I'm sorry, Domingo," she said. "You're quite right. I overdid it."

"Keep it up and I'll schedule an extra hour's rehearsal every day," he threatened, and she laughed and told him she wouldn't mind that a bit.

MICHAEL WAS WAITING in the restaurant lobby. "You were great tonight," he said, opening the door for her. She had to pass close by him, close enough to smell the clean scent of him, almost close enough to brush against him. The air outside felt charged with danger. What had happened to her anger? Had she sung it all out? She had to dredge it up again fast.

"Nobody rushed up to Domingo to congratulate him on his new discovery," she said dryly.

"They will. The response was good. Not over-whelming, but then response to a new singer seldom is."

He was walking along beside her to the parking area. She switched the bag containing her jeans and T-shirt into the hand next to him, creating a barrier.

"Blythe," he protested softly.

She turned to face him. "You don't have to take me home," she said. "I drove myself over. I'll drive myself back."

"Are you telling me we're no longer friends?"

"I'm telling you to leave me alone."

He turned to regard her with unconcealed inter-est. "Why? Are you afraid you won't be able to re-sist me?"

When she wasn't being attracted to this man, she was totally exasperated by him. "How can you think such a thing?" she demanded. "Especially after you told me...suggested—" She broke off, aware of the utter impossibility of repeating the things he'd said.

"I think you want me as much as I want you," he said as though he were merely repeating a well-known fact.

Speechless, she stared at him. He looked back at her directly. Then he shook his head, took her arm and urged her toward his car. She stood her ground, her body rigid, fighting a desire to yell at him, to tell him she most certainly did not want him in any way.

When she refused to budge, he glanced at her with a coaxing little smile. "I just want to apologize," he said in a humble voice, and she was so surprised by his sudden reversal that she allowed him to help her into the passenger seat as though she were a doll stuffed with rags, unable to control her own limbs.

"I'm so damned attracted to you it scares me," he said after he'd walked around the car and seated himself behind the wheel. There was a disarming expression of humility on his face. "I think I told you I used to be the class clown in school. My father used to get furious with me for what he called wisecracking, when all the time I was covering up for feelings I couldn't deal with. I do the same thing with you. I have to pretend my feelings for you aren't serious, you see, because if I tell you they are and you reject me, as seems most likely in the face of your attachment to Craig, then I'd be devastated."

She stared at him in the dimness of the car, wishing she could see his facial expression more clearly. She wasn't sure if he was mocking her again, or if he really meant what he was saying.

A sudden, totally unexpected and mischievous idea occurred to her. There was one way to find out if he was still performing a charade. She made her face and voice deliberately grave. "Are you saying that you do want me to marry you after all?" she asked.

He kept his poise admirably; she had to give him that. Only the swift intake of his breath told her she'd rocked him. "Well, that's certainly one option," he said slowly.

"Is there another?"

She should have been warned by the sudden gleam in his dark eyes. Even in the dim light she was able to see that. But she was so caught up in her own cleverness in tricking him that she didn't realize he was more than a match for her until she was in his arms, being thoroughly kissed and responding just as readily as she had the previous night.

There seemed to be a time lapse. Some minutes later she found herself giving in to an earlier desire, finger-combing his hair as he trailed a line of kisses across her throat. His hair felt as wonderful as she'd imagined. Thick and crisp and clean, it clung to her fingers with a vigor of its own. "Mmm." She sighed.

He raised his head, and she saw the flash of his smile in the dark. "Beautiful Blythe," he said softly. And then his mouth covered hers again, and her fingers stilled as she gave herself up to the supreme pleasure of his kiss.

His arms were around her, clasping her lightly. She wanted to press herself against him, but a residual shyness held her back. And then she realized why he hadn't pressed her too close...his left hand was traveling down her body, coming dangerously near her breast. And she had no wish to stop his light exploration. It seemed the most natural thing in the world for him to cup her breast in his long-fingered hand, to brush his thumb lightly across the nipple, teasing it erect without any effort at all. One part of her brain was alert, though, ready to stop him if his fingers showed any inclination to slide toward the zipper that ran the length of the jump suit. Madness this might be and irresistible the man, but Blythe was not one to get completely carried away.

He made no attempt to go further, but contented himself with stroking her breast lightly, maddeningly, while his mouth showed her new ways to communicate pleasure. She had never realized how thoroughly a mouth could make love. His lips were now stern, now pliant, now brushing lightly, now pressing against hers while his tongue, curled to just the right amount for comfort, explored the roof of her mouth, the inner tissues of her cheeks, the cool smooth surfaces of her teeth.

While her breath quickened until she thought she would hyperventilate, while her pulse hammered in her chest, her throat, her head, she could still admire his skill, his dedication to the kisses that he seemed in no hurry to end. She could also admire, with her fingertips, the firm contours of the slim male body beneath the light gabardine jacket, the tight smooth muscles that were so neatly contained in his skin. There wasn't a noticeable bulge anywhere on his upper body. Yet there was no mistaking his strength. He could have crushed her easily. But instead he continued to hold her lightly, gently, as though he were telling her with body language that she was free to break his embrace at any moment.

After what seemed a long, long time, yet not quite long enough, he lifted his head away from her. "I have an idea this sort of thing doesn't happen very often," he said softly, and she thrilled to the spaces between his words that told her he was having trouble breathing himself.

"What?" she asked.

"This total meshing of biological urges. Like two half bodies that have found their counterparts at last."

He was being facetious again, and she wasn't quite ready for humor. "It sounds very clinical," she said.

He laughed shortly. "Sex always does when you talk about it."

Sex.

Maybe he was right about her, Blythe thought. Maybe she was one of those women who expected every relationship to end in a proposal of marriage. Though the idea of being married to Michael Channing was ludicrous. Any wife of his would be gray-haired before she was thirty. If he was one minute late from work, she'd want to know not if he'd been with another woman, but what her name was. She'd be that sure he was cheating.

"You're remarkably silent, sweet Blythe," he said.

She managed a very weak imitation of laughter. She had to keep this light. She couldn't let him know she'd come close to taking him at his word and treating what was between them seriously. Most important of all, she had to avoid giving him any opportunity to kiss her again. "I'm just trying to get my breath back," she said in a breezy voice she hadn't heard herself use before.

His laugh was genuine. "We can't have that, can we?" he murmured, and he was kissing her again, scattering all her good intentions to the wind.

"Maybe we can't be just friends," he said dolefully while she was still trying to compose herself after yet another lapse of time. Then he looked at her very intently. "If you don't get out of here in one second flat, I won't answer for the consequences," he announced.

As she tried to marshal her chaotic emotions, hoping to come up with an answer that would set him firmly in his place once and for all, he kissed her nose lightly, leaned across her and opened the door. "I'll just watch to be sure you get away safely," he said.

Dumbfounded, she had no choice but to scramble awkwardly out of his car.

"See you tomorrow, Daisy," he called after her.

She'd left the car door open, and he had to slide over to pull it shut. Afraid she'd sputter if she tried to say anything, she glared at him as he poked his head out of the half-open door. "I love you in that jump suit," he said. "You look like a particularly curvaceous lollipop. A strawberry lollipop."

In the next moment, he'd started the BMW and driven out of the parking lot, apparently forgetting his promise to watch her leave.

Blythe stared after the car long after it left, the imprint of its taillights flashing in front of her eyes like twin beacons. Her emotions were so completely jumbled that she had no idea which one was uppermost. The man was impossible, unreal. She must have made him up, like one of the fantasies he was so fond of. A dream lover to drive her mad so she could sing with more emotion. Or maybe her brain, bored with its own practicality and common sense, had conjured him up to provide her life with some comic relief. Turning toward her own car, she started to laugh, but a minute later, as she turned the key in the ignition, she stopped laughing and found herself putting her fingers to her lips. They felt bruised, tender, swollen with sweet memory.

Michael Channing was real all right, and she was in mortal danger of losing her head and her heart unless she was very, very careful.

5

MICHAEL HAD SAID, "See you tomorrow," but he didn't come to the Starlight on Sunday. Blythe decided business must have called him away, though he'd never seemed too serious about business. On Monday she thought perhaps he'd had to go out of town, or perhaps he just wasn't interested in appearing at rehearsals. By Friday she was seething with anger, at him and at herself, beginning to suspect he'd disappeared from her life as abruptly as he'd come into it. Still, she found herself scanning the audience all weekend—to no avail.

She didn't hear from him during the following week, and she learned the tyranny that could be exerted by a telephone. When it rang she felt a thrill of anticipation, followed by deep disappointment when the caller wasn't him. In the office, every time the door opened, she looked up expectantly, her pulse quickening, and when she drove a tour she searched the assembled group for that familiar shock of black hair.

"Yeah, he comes around pretty often," Domingo said when she questioned him casually. "He's not the absentee-landlord type. He likes to keep tabs on things. Maybe one of the other restaurants has some problems." He looked at her sharply. "You aren't getting the hots for him, are you?"

She felt herself flushing, but managed to laugh.

"You're about as subtle as a ton of bricks, Dom," she said with apparent ease. Then she shook her head. "I was just curious."

"Uh-huh." He fingered a chord, then looked at her under his eyelashes. "I wouldn't get too involved, babe. That's a dude who believes there's safety in numbers."

"So I've heard."

Domingo nodded and didn't volunteer anything more.

At least one problem had been solved for her, Blythe told herself in an attempt to ignore her growing disillusionment. She didn't have to worry anymore that Michael Channing would come between her and Craig. She'd really had a lucky escape, and it was silly to feel disappointed that Michael had turned out to be the lightweight she'd first thought him. She'd expected him to let her down, hadn't she? Even while she was losing her head over him. It had been perfectly obvious from the start that he looked upon her as a light diversion, someone he could amuse himself with. A project, perhaps, in the tradition of *My Fair Lady*. He'd wanted to play Henry Higgins to her Eliza; that was all. Still, she couldn't deny the persistent pain that kept nagging somewhere inside her.

She also had problems with Craig. Though he'd made no further objection to her singing, he kept insisting he needed time alone with her. And David had evidently been primed to help him achieve this object. Every time Blythe came home from rehearsal, David took himself off on a date with Stephanie Goodwin, very obviously leaving her alone with Craig. She had to quickly think up some problem with the bookkeeping and occupy Craig with that until it was late enough to plead fatigue.

She couldn't understand her reluctance to be alone with Craig. It was as though she couldn't let him touch her as long as her feelings for Michael were still unsettled. But they *were* settled, she tried to tell herself. Michael had settled them for her by disappearing. Surely she wasn't hanging on to some forlorn hope that he'd come around soon, that he'd turn up with a perfectly acceptable excuse for his absence and would want to start up with her again where he had left off?

By the last Friday of her trial period, she decided Michael had definitely given up on her. His interest in her had lasted for exactly a week after Julie's wedding—which Craig had told her at the start was standard for him. His protestations of serious involvement had obviously been part of a seduction package that he'd decided not to follow up on.

Thinking that as long as she was safe now, she might as well try to involve Craig in her new venture, she invited David and him to come to the Starlight Room for the Friday-night session, promising to pay for their drinks and cover charge out of her earnings. She soon regretted her invitation. When she brought Domingo over to their table during the first break, Craig barely acknowledged the introduction. "Do you have to move around so much?" he hissed at her in a harsh voice she'd never heard come out of him before.

"Sure she does," Domingo said promptly. "She's only dancing. What you got against dancing?"

"I didn't like you jumping around up there in front of everybody," Craig continued, ignoring Domingo altogether.

Domingo didn't like to be ignored. "You want her

to jump around between the tables, man?" he asked loudly.

"I was hardly jumping around, Craig," Blythe protested. "All I did was sway a little in time to the music."

"Well, it looked damn suggestive." She hadn't noticed before that Craig's jaw could jut out quite so far. Conscious that the people at the next table were delightedly eavesdropping, she murmured something soothing and evasive in an attempt to calm him down.

But then Domingo muttered a few words that ended with, *"el squaro,"* and she was pretty sure Craig heard. She felt defensive, wanted to tell Domingo that Craig was usually gregarious, fun loving. But annoyed herself with the way Craig was behaving, she didn't say anything and immediately felt guilty. He could at least smile, she thought after she returned to the stage and started singing again. He could at least pretend he was enjoying himself.

And then she looked out into the audience and saw Michael Channing sitting at one of the little tables near the stage. To her dismay, she felt an immediate jolt in the region of her heart. Her spirits, which had sunk gradually over the past two weeks like a soufflé left too long out of the oven, revived miraculously. Somehow she managed to keep on singing.

In the next instant she noticed that he wasn't alone. He was accompanied by a woman of about forty who was dressed in an elegant black-silk tunic and pants, with twisted red-and-gold scarves in lieu of a belt and yards of funky jewelry around her neck. Her hair was as black as his, but tortured into masses of curls that writhed around her face in Medusalike coils. She was surveying the crowded room as though she owned the place and was counting heads so she could calculate the evening's take.

Michael was ignoring the woman, looking at Blythe in his usual quizzical way, his gaze barely shifting from her for a moment. She had a horrible premonition that when the group broke for the second time, he'd come over to Craig's table and make things worse between the two of them. Yet at the same time she felt unmistakably overjoyed that Michael was there, that he'd come back. Which showed how truly stupid she could be. Even though he was watching her as admiringly as always, he'd obviously found a new woman for this week...an older, *responsible* woman. With an effort, she looked away from him and concentrated on her singing.

She had begun to sing "Come to Me," wishing she'd told Domingo that she was sure it would work better as the duet it was supposed to be. She didn't yet feel competent enough to make suggestions when they discussed an evening's program. It sounded okay, she thought, but the song really needed two voices.

Even as she thought this, she heard another voice join hers from behind and was startled to realize it was Eddie who had come in. He rarely sang backup, and then only in the rock numbers. His voice was pleasant, unremarkable, occasionally monotonous, but combined with hers it gave the song an added dimension, more texture, a vibrantly erotic sound that thrilled her.

She was obviously not alone in her reaction. One by one, heads started turning. Suddenly the dancers were looking at the stage rather than at their partners. Domingo was glancing from her to Eddie with a delighted grin, nodding to encourage them both to continue. Electricity was in the air. When the song ended, the audience applauded vigorously. Even Craig was leaning forward, clapping as hard as anyone. Michael was sitting very straight, looking directly at her with a wry, "I-told-you-so," expression on his face. The woman with him had stopped looking around the room, but she was the one exception to the general excitement. Her eyes were on Blythe, but she looked bored and disinterested.

Blythe caught Michael's gaze while she waited for the next intro, and he raised one hand and gave her a signal of approval, thumb and forefinger joined. Immediately she forgot about the woman with him, forgot that he'd deserted her, forgot all her warnings to herself. She felt a rush of satisfaction and achievement and happiness that she had never experienced before.

She and Eddie sang three more songs together, and the sound was just as rich and mellow and exciting. And then, even more remarkably, when she sang the next song alone, she somehow retained the feeling Eddie had generated and discovered a new huskiness in the lower ranges of her voice that gave it an added depth of its own.

At the break, Domingo punched Eddie's shoulder and hugged Blythe and told them they were spectacular. "We're gonna rehearse the pants off both of you tomorrow," he said. "We've got something really different here, and we have to try it out on our own stuff and see how it sounds." Turning to Blythe, he added, "Wherever you got that smoky sound, hang on to it. That's the new Blythe Sherwood, and she's a winner all the way."

Craig was almost as enthusiastic. "You sounded fantastic," he said as she sat down.

Relieved that he'd come around again, she leaned over and kissed him on the cheek, still caught up in the excitement herself. He looked even more pleased.

"Looks as though Eddie's your new twin," David said. He was grinning, but something had flickered in his eyes that told her he wasn't altogether joking.

"One twin's all I need," she assured him, and his smile spread to his eyes.

And then the moment she'd dreaded was suddenly upon her. She felt a hand on her shoulder, to which her body responded even before she looked up to see that it did indeed belong to Michael. "May I join you?" he asked.

He was looking at Dave, and her brother answered, "Sure" in his always-friendly manner before she or Craig could object. That Craig did object was obvious. He at once retreated back into the shell that had come over him earlier.

"Wouldn't you like to invite your friend to sit with us?" Blythe asked. She hadn't meant to emphasize the word "friend," but it came out that way and Michael's eyebrows formed a puzzled inverted vee.

A moment later his brow cleared. "Oh, you mean Mrs. Berenstein."

"*Mrs.* Berenstein?"

"A business acquaintance," he explained with a charming smile. "She had to leave." Unexpectedly he put an arm around Blythe's shoulders and hugged her exuberantly, exclaiming, "I'm excited about your performance. All that fire. I knew it was there. I knew you could be great." His dark eyes gleaming with intensity, he went on, "The hair stood up on the back of my neck when you and Eddie started singing together. And when you sang the last song alone, someone nearby asked, 'Who *is* she?'"

He gave her a cheerful grin. "I told him your name used to be Daisy, but now you were known as Blythe Sherwood."

"Why the hell would you say that?" Craig demanded. He had sat through the preceding minutes as stiffly as though his spine were a steel rod; his mouth was set in an ominous line.

Blythe's heart turned over. She could quite cheerfully have strangled Michael on the spot. But he wasn't fazed for a second. "Just building a legend," he told Craig airily. "Every celebrity has to have a legend."

"Blythe's hardly a celebrity," Craig said.

Michael's irrepressible eyebrows slanted upward. "She is as far as I'm concerned." He hugged her once more, then released her. "I'm expecting all kinds of great things of you now."

"She's only going to be singing two more nights," Craig said.

Michael looked at her questioningly, and when she didn't, couldn't respond, directed his suddenly cool gaze at Craig. "What makes you say that?"

"Blythe promised me she wouldn't sing here for more than two weeks."

"Craig," Blythe protested, but then Domingo tapped her on the shoulder and she had to leave.

For the rest of the evening, she was conscious of Michael's looking at her with questions in his eyes. When the time came to go home, she could see he wanted to detain her, but she managed covertly to shake her head, and he stood aside and watched her go by with Craig and David without saying a word.

MURMURING, "THE BETTER PART OF VALOR IS DISCRETION," David took himself off to bed the moment they arrived at the apartment, leaving her alone with Craig.

She sat next to him on the sofa, realizing, in spite of her annoyance with him, that when his face creased in the earnest lines that meant he was sure he was in the right, he was at his most lovable.

All the same, she wasn't going to back down. He had behaved badly, like a spoiled little boy, and she intended to tell him so.

Looking at him, exasperated, she suddenly realized that the *reasonable* expression on his face was familiar. Five years ago, he'd worn this expression when he sat her down in her sorority living room and proposed that she switch to business courses, instead of sticking with her music. She'd agreed it was a sensible thing to do. He hadn't really pressured her, but he had managed to make her feel guilty about studying music when she and David had to make their own way. David had added to the pressure. He had been immediately enthusiastic about the prospect of the three of them going into business together. How could she not have agreed?

For a moment she could barely breathe. For five years she'd thought the decision to switch majors was her own, and she had always been proud of her good sense. But it was suddenly clear to her that she'd merely given in to pressure. Craig and even David had manipulated her.

It was a stunning realization, but it was too late now to make any accusations about the past. All the same, she was alerted—she wasn't going to let Craig deflect her from her true course this time. But before speaking, she forced herself to push all resentment down. After all, she did enjoy the tour business, and she loved working with David and Craig. It was just that sometimes she felt that life was going by and she was only existing, not really living, that there had to be more....

"I didn't make any promises about not singing after Sunday," she said carefully. "You asked me to promise, and I refused. I was very angry tonight when you made it appear I'd decided to quit."

"But, Blythe, it's obviously too much for you. Look how tired you get...always wanting to go to bed early. You were a nervous wreck last weekend, and you'll probably be the same tomorrow. You have the La Jolla trip tomorrow so you don't have to get up quite so early, but even so you won't get enough sleep. And Sunday—"

"The reason I'm so tired," she interrupted hotly, "is because I've been working doubly hard the past two weeks so you and Dave wouldn't feel I was neglecting the business. I've done more than my share of meals and laundry and...."

"We didn't ask you to do extra," Craig pointed out reasonably and truthfully.

"I know that. But I felt it was necessary to prove that I was still capable—" She broke off. "Why the hell should I be made to feel guilty because I'm singing three nights a week and enjoying it?"

"Nobody can make you feel guilty, Blythe. Such emotions are self-induced."

"Don't quote Psych 101 to me," she snapped.

He sighed audibly. "We're fighting again," he said sadly, unnecessarily.

"No, we're not. I'm through fighting. And I'm through overcompensating. And if Domingo asks me to stay on, I'll make my own decision, without any help from you or David."

"I guess I'll have to accept that, then," he said carefully.

"I guess you will," she answered. She hesitated, feeling drained, wanting the discussion to be over so she could get some sleep. "I'm sorry it upsets you, Craig, but I do enjoy singing. I feel now that I can be pretty good."

He had turned his head away again and was looking down at his hands, clasped together between his legs. It was a defeated attitude that never failed to soften her. She felt herself softening now. "I've never felt so vigorous, so alive as I do when I'm singing," she added quietly.

"You don't feel alive when you're being a tour guide?" he asked with a crookedly endearing smile.

"Is there any reason I can't be both?"

He touched her lips with his fingers, tracing their outlines, his fingers gentle. "I've been a bastard, haven't I?" he said, and she melted totally, won over by his disarming admission.

A moment later she allowed him to take her in his arms. But she couldn't bring herself to let her lips meet his. Guilt over Michael Channing was getting in the way of her feelings for Craig, deep feelings that had been tested over almost ten years, not transitory physical responses such as those Michael aroused in her. Yet somehow she couldn't seem to relax with Craig as she always had. "I'm too tired," she told him.

He said he understood, but then he added, in what was evidently supposed to be a peacemaking gesture, that he really didn't object to her singing as long as she didn't neglect the tour business...or him. Which seemed to foreshadow more problems. She sighed inwardly. She couldn't bring herself to

Harlequin Temptation™

Have you ever thought
you were in love
with one man...only
to feel attracted to another?

That's just one of the temptations you'll find facing the women in *Harlequin Temptation* romance novels.

Sensuous ... contemporary ... compelling ... reflecting today's love relationships!

The passionate torment of a woman torn between two loves...the siren call of a career...the magnetic advances of an impetuous employer—nothing is left unexplored in this romantic series from Harlequin. You'll thrill to a candid new frankness as men and women seek to form lasting relationships in the face of temptations that threaten true love. *Don't miss a single one!* You can start *Harlequin Temptation* coming to your home each month for just $1.75 per book. Begin with your FREE copy of *First Impressions*.

Mail the reply card today!

GET THIS BOOK FREE!

First Impressions
by Maris Soule

He was involved with her best friend. Tracy Dexter couldn't deny her attraction to her new boss. Mark Prescott looked more like a jet set playboy than a high school principal—and he acted like one, too. It wasn't right for Tracy to go out with him, not when her friend Rose had already staked a claim. It wasn't right, even though Mark's eyes were so persuasive, his kiss so probing and intense. Even though his hands scorched her body with a teasing, raging fire...and when he gently lowered her to the floor she couldn't find the words to say no.

A word of warning to our regular readers: While Harlequin books are always in good taste, you'll find more sensuous writing in *Harlequin Temptation* than in other Harlequin romance series.

® ™ Trademarks of Harlequin Enterprises Ltd.

worry about the future now. It was all she could do to keep up with the present.

MICHAEL CORNERED HER midway through Saturday's rehearsal, as she'd half expected him to. When she stopped for a break, he sat her down and pulled up a chair next to her and said, "Okay, Daisy, give. What's this about two more nights and that's it?"

"Please don't call me 'Daisy,'" she said tiredly. "I've had enough of arguing. I'm not afraid," she added before he could ask whom she'd been arguing with. "I have to decide which priorities are most important to me. It doesn't help when you call me 'Daisy' and accuse me of running away or hiding or whatever."

"Domingo *is* going to ask you to stay on," Michael said softly.

She stared at him. "He told you that?"

He nodded. "I've kept in touch with him. He's delighted with your progress." He hesitated. "What are you going to tell him?"

She laughed shortly, feeling a surge of pleasure in spite of her worries. "I guess that I'm going to keep on singin'."

He leaned forward and kissed her swiftly on the mouth before she could object. "That's my girl," he said warmly, and she felt a tremor of fear go through her as her heart leaped in answer to his kiss.

He was looking at her very sheepishly now, which was unusual for him. "I guess I've been imitating Daisy myself," he said softly.

"You deliberately stayed away?"

He nodded. "I have this health problem," he said solemnly.

"You were sick?"

"Not exactly. The nature of my ailment is terminal cold feet. It comes over me whenever I feel myself getting too close to a woman. The usual cure is abrupt disentanglement."

"I haven't entangled you," she said stiffly.

"I didn't say you had. The entanglement is all my own doing."

"Why did you come back at all, then?"

His eyes met hers, and there was a glint in them that told her she was about to be teased again. Her heart lifted with an absurd little bump.

"I remembered that I'd promised to teach you to believe in fairy tales."

She swallowed. "Fairy tales have nothing to do with real life."

"You don't think it's something of a fairy tale that you are singing here?"

"I suppose it has its fairy-tale aspects, and I'm grateful—"

"I don't want gratitude," he said firmly.

"What do you want, then?"

His eyes met hers, gleaming, both eyebrows slanting irrepressibly. He touched her lips with the fingers of one hand, then ran his thumb gently across her mouth and sighed theatrically. What he wanted was obvious.

She felt her knees disintegrating, and she stood up abruptly. "You're incorrigible," she told him as she'd told him before. "It's only in stories that the princess goes off with the prince into the sunset."

"But you want to, don't you?" he said promptly.

Helplessly she felt her senses responding to the wicked smile that had accompanied his suggestion. Her whole body was suddenly yearning for him. She wanted to touch him, to take his hand and walk

with him out of the building, out onto the Embarcadero. They would stand for a while admiring all the
lights—those on Harbor Island in the near distance
reflecting like brightly colored pillars reaching down
to the seabed, the paler necklace of lights outlining
the Coronado Bay Bridge, boat lights moving like
fireflies across the calm rippling water. After a
while, he would put his arms around her and kiss
her and hold her, their bodies silhouetted against the
night sky.

Bemused by the images she'd conjured up, she
managed to shake her head again. The whole scene
might have been lifted from some sentimental movie,
and at any moment the words "The End" would be
superimposed over the two lovers. "I'm not admitting
any such thing," she said firmly.

"You will," he said cheerfully. He was still smiling
confidently as she walked away.

DOMINGO PRESENTED A COUPLE OF NEW SONGS at the end of
the evening that she hadn't yet had a chance to rehearse. She stood back from the microphone and
listened, trying to memorize the words and melody.
As she stood there at the side of the stage tapping
one foot, she saw Michael walking toward her. He
had disappeared by the time rehearsal was over and
hadn't returned until a few minutes ago. She had
noticed him the second he entered the room and had
felt a return of the trepidation he invariably elicited
in her. Singing her last song, conscious of his decep-
tively lazy dark gaze, she had felt as though something were ticking away inside her, a metronome, or
a clock. She had known the instant he returned that
he would wait for her after everyone left. And she
would have to make a decision that could affect her

whole future, a decision she wasn't yet ready to make.

He looked up at her with his usual quizzical smile. "Would you like to dance?" he asked.

She glanced at Domingo as though she expected him to tell her what to do, but he was engrossed in his music, one foot propped on the stool he always kept on the stage, his head bent over his guitar.

"I guess I could," she said doubtfully. After all, the dance floor was a public place. He could hardly be a problem to her there.

Which showed, she thought almost immediately, that she must still have been caught up in Domingo's music and neither her memory nor her brain were functioning properly. Because as soon as she stepped down from the stage she knew what was going to happen. But by then it was too late.

She was in his arms, feeling as though she belonged there. The music was all around them...one of Domingo's more romantic ballads. And once again she had stepped into another dimension. The crowded dance floor had receded into some kind of mist. No one else was really there at all. The other couples were wraiths dancing in a parody of Walt Disney's haunted mansion...unsubstantial, unreal. And after all, there was no need to make a decision. Somewhere deep in her subconscious mind it had already been made.

HE HELD HER HAND while he drove, and he talked cheerfully for a while, not giving her time to think, summarizing every fairy tale she'd ever heard and a few she hadn't run into, explaining their meanings to her, the lessons that could be drawn from them. "I've never thought about a fairy tale as a psychological treatise before," she said with a laugh.

"Most of them are moral tales," he pointed out. "A mixture of idealism and bitterness, like life. Each one has its own message: 'The Ugly Duckling,' 'The Emperor's New Clothes.' Fairy tales are good for us, especially in this century with its overtones of nightmare fantasy. As long as we can believe that Jack can defeat the giant and—" he directed a sidelong smile at her "—that Rapunzel will eventually let down her long hair, we can face getting up tomorrow with equanimity, or even with joy."

"Not many people talk about joy," Blythe murmured.

He lifted her hand to his lips and kissed it tenderly. "That's what I've been trying to tell you," he answered.

She gazed at his strong profile for a time without speaking, wondering if he meant her to believe fantasy was better than real life, or that a certain amount of fantasy was necessary in order to enjoy real life. Perhaps there was more to this man than she'd realized. She found herself thinking about artichokes—leaves within leaves within leaves. Then laughed at her fancy. He raised an eyebrow at her, but she refused to explain her laughter. "You wouldn't be flattered," she assured him.

For a short time they drove in silence, and there was even a fantasy element to this silent racing through the night, headlights illuminating the endless ribbon of yellow that bisected the road. Buildings rushed by them, and huge palms and eucalyptus trees and street signs and occasionally other cars. To their left, down side streets, she now and then caught a glimpse of the endless dark of the sea.

Inside the car was only the purr of the motor, the hum of tires on asphalt, the faint rustle of clothing as one of them moved slightly. Tension was there,

too, building in the silence, quickening Blythe's
breathing, tightening Michael's grip on her hand.
Soon they would arrive at Michael's house in La
Jolla, prepared to embark on a new journey into an
unexplored land.

BLYTHE STOOD BEFORE THE CATHEDRAL WINDOW of Michael's living room looking down at the darkly
shimmering Pacific with its ghostly frilled edge of
waves gently creaming against the sandy beach,
imagining the magnificent view there must be in the
daytime. Her parents' house had been situated not
too far from here, just beyond the next promontory
but set back from the sea. She had loved that house.
And La Jolla.

"The jewel" of the Pacific. How often had she told
her tourists the translation of the name of what must
surely be one of the loveliest beach towns anywhere? Everything in La Jolla had to be described in
superlatives... the bluest water, the grandest homes,
the best hotels, restaurants, art galleries....

"What are you thinking?" Michael asked from
behind her.

She looked at his reflection in the dark glass and
saw that he'd removed his suit jacket and tie, opened
the collar of his white shirt. In the process he'd managed to tousle his hair. She smiled, letting out a
breath she hadn't realized she was holding. "I was
thinking about La Jolla. I used to live here."

"And would like to move back?"

She hesitated, considering. "I don't know. Maybe
I've grown away from it. I really enjoy the touristy
bustle of San Diego."

They were making talk, she realized. The tension
that had grown between them earlier hadn't dissi-

pated at all since they entered this soaring modernistic house, even though Blythe had experienced the oddest sensation of homecoming when she walked into the huge living room, with its made-for-comfort chairs and sofas, its gleaming wood and glass tables and mahogany-framed fireplace, the brilliantly colored contemporary art displayed on the stark white walls, the fine stone sculptures.

"Blythe," Michael said tentatively.

She turned around to face him, surprised. He was not in any way a tentative man. Yet now he looked almost uncertain in the light cast by the hanging lamps he'd switched on. His hands were held straight at his sides, fists lightly clenched.

"Michael," she said, echoing his solemn tone of voice, teasing him though her own hands were clasped behind her back in what was probably white-knuckled intensity.

He didn't smile. Something was bothering him. A frown was furrowing his forehead between those impossibly slanted eyebrows. "I haven't ever believed it's possible for a man to steal a woman from another man," he said slowly. "The concept implies that the woman is a possession." He hesitated. "All the same, there is a certain aspect to our situation that makes me afraid I might be stealing *something.*"

Blythe swallowed, feeling a sudden stab of guilt at the reminder of Craig. "I thought of you as a thief when I first met you," she said after a moment, trying and failing to speak lightly.

He looked startled.

"I don't mean a real thief," she hastened to explain. "I thought of you as the very best kind of Hollywood movie burglar . . . the kind who steals diamond necklaces from the most beautiful women at a house party in an elegant mansion. The kind of sexy thief women are flattered to lose their jewelry to."

He didn't smile. "I'm not sure if that's a compliment or an insult."

Blythe laughed a little breathlessly. There was still the most extraordinary tension between them, almost a palpable barrier. "Perhaps you'd like my other idea better...I also saw you as 007."

One eyebrow lifted. "As played by Sean Connery or Roger Moore?" he asked.

"A combination of both."

"I see."

Silence again. He was waiting for an answer to his implied question. Blythe took a deep breath. "Craig has never actually asked me to marry him," she said evenly. "It was understood between us, though. And I do find myself feeling guilty about the way I've been treating him."

"But?"

"At the same time, he never has made any definite promises or commitments or even declarations."

"Have you?"

"No."

Was he going to ask if she loved Craig? How would she answer? At this moment she didn't know the answer.

He didn't ask. His usual intent gaze had brightened as they spoke. His eyes were gleaming now with a dark amusement she felt was directed more at himself and his need for reassurance than at her. Obviously he hadn't wanted to admit he was an honorable man. Was he afraid such an admission would spoil his rakish image?

"What about you?" she asked in a halting voice.

"You were married. I understand you walked out on your wife."

He looked beyond her at the dark window glass, then nodded. "Yes, I did."

"For no reason?" When he failed to answer, she let out her breath. "You must see, Michael, that if that's the way it was it's hardly a recommendation. How do I know you won't do the same to me right after...?" She swallowed. "For all I know, you could still be in love with your wife."

"I'm not." There was such steely conviction in his voice, such coldness in his clipped reply that she shivered.

"I'm not a promiscuous woman," she said lamely. "I don't offer my... *friendship* lightly."

He smiled faintly at the euphemism, then looked at her directly. Something was gone from his usual expression—warmth, vitality—as though a shutter had come down over a camera lens, closing out the light.

"I wasn't trying to evade your question," he said at last. "I've never talked to anyone about what happened between Ellie and me. It's not easy." His mouth tightened at one corner and he glanced away from her again, drew in a deep breath, then met her gaze once more. "I can't talk about it, Blythe." His eyes held a look now that was almost pleading. There was pain there, too. Whatever the reason for the breakup of his marriage, he had suffered over it. In the face of his obvious anguish, she couldn't press him to explain.

She sighed. "I guess I'll just have to take a chance, then," she said softly.

He nodded solemnly. "I can't promise that what's between us will last forever," he said slowly. "I be-

lieve I told you that I'm only an amateur when it
comes to fortune-telling." He took another deep
breath, then smiled more naturally. "I can promise I
won't walk out on you tomorrow. In spite of my du-
bious reputation, I'm not in favor of one-night
stands."

For another minute or so they stood looking at
each other, still not moving toward each other
through that invisible barrier that was as strong as a
force field keeping apart two like magnetic poles.
"I'm having the most awful problem," he confided
after another short silence. He paused for a heartbeat's time, then swallowed visibly. "I'm afraid if I
touch you I'm going to explode."

Blythe's mouth was suddenly dry, but she returned his gaze steadily. "In that case, I have a problem, too," she told him.

His eyes narrowed.

"If you *don't* touch me, *I'm* going to explode."

Then they were both laughing, and the invisible
barrier shattered into millions of harmless particles
of air. His arms were around her and hers around
him, and he was kissing her hungrily, his mouth
warm and tender on hers, his hands stroking her
firmly, gently, down from her shoulders to her
waist, again and again. Her own hands were cupping his face, reveling in the slight rasp of his skin
against the smooth surface of her palms.

When she'd thought about being seduced by Michael, and she had, she'd half expected him to come
on with a line of slick bright patter that would dis-
tract her from whatever he was doing to her body.
But he surprised her. There wasn't even a hint of
seduction. Not a sly glance or a loaded metaphor or
even a direct request. He simply took her hand after

nearly kissing her breath away and led her into the bedroom. He even let her undress herself while he took his own clothes off, smiling at her, not talking at all. Also surprisingly, she felt no embarrassment, even though there was enough brightness shining through from the globular lights in the hall to show both their bodies fairly clearly. Always with Craig, she had worried that she wouldn't be able to please him. With Michael, she found herself anticipating in a totally hedonistic way how much he was going to please her.

She was glad that he let his clothes fall where he took them off. Though a tidy person herself, she'd always felt uncomfortable while she waited for Craig to hang his slacks just so over a chair back so that they wouldn't get wrinkled. And she'd always compulsively copied Craig, folding her own clothing in a neat pile as she might in a doctor's examining room, hiding her panties and bra inside her other garments, often wishing she had the doctor's paper gown to pull over her while she waited for Craig to get through lining up his shoes and piling up the change he'd taken from his trouser pockets.

The shocking-pink jump suit was an easy garment to remove. She followed it with her wispy bra and bikini underpants and stood quite unself-consciously while Michael looked at her, smiling his approval. His own body owed nothing to the cut of his clothes for its trim appearance. He was slim in the right places, broad in the shoulders, tapered at the hips. His suntan ended at the line of his shorts. Just as unself-consciously, he stood still a moment, letting her look at him, admire him, letting her see for herself that he desired her tremendously.

Then he reached to pull down the covers and she

helped fold them down, and then, still without embarrassment, she was on the bed and he was holding her close while she gasped out her surprise. The bed was warm. And it moved.

"A water bed?" she said unbelievingly.

His lips grazed her forehead. "I know it seems too much of a playboy cliché, but it's really very comfortable. A chiropractor friend recommended it to me when I sprained my back skiing a couple of years ago."

"It's marvelous," Blythe exclaimed, experimenting with gentle bounces, laughing.

"So are you," Michael murmured.

There was no more laughter then. His mouth met hers and passion exploded between them just as they'd both expected. He was all around her, hands stroking downward again, his mouth following his hands, smoothing her body as though it were molded of clay fired in a kiln and had to be polished to the fine sheen of porcelain. He touched every part of her, parts she had never expected to be explored, as though he wanted her to know that he enjoyed every inch of her, from her toes to her thighs to her breasts and shoulder blades and even the smooth warm places under her arms.

She explored him just as wantonly, the two of them moving easily, automatically, to provide access to each other, the bed supporting and aiding them by providing an undulating surface that rolled with them and closed around them in its own warm embrace.

He didn't seem to tire of kissing her. And his mouth was so inventive, so pleasure giving and pleasure seeking that Blythe was enchanted by it and thought she could never have enough.

Their movements seemed so well timed, so well fitted to each other that they might have been rehearsed beforehand. There was never a moment's awkwardness or hesitation. His hands fitted her breasts exactly. Hip to hip their flat stomachs matched like two halves of the same whole. The top of her head fitted into the underside of his chin. And when he moved his head lower to touch his delicately curled tongue to first the smooth wide areola of her breast and then one erect nipple, her hands cupped the shape of his head as though the curve of it had been programmed into them.

His hair felt wonderful to her, strong and vigorous and alive. She marveled at the erotic sensations he aroused in her when he slid down even lower and his hair brushed the honey blond triangle that protected her most private domain. Even while one detached part of her brain examined these sensations, his tongue teased her to heights of passion she had never reached, even in fantasy, and she felt her whole body tightening and lifting, arching to him and the pleasure he was giving her, straining upward in a tension that seemed unbearable, *was* unbearable...a high-pitched, hand-clenching, glorious tension that suddenly exploded all around her.

At once he moved to hold her, and she clutched him mindlessly until her pulse finally slowed and the breath came back to her body and her blood lessened its reckless progress through her heart.

He murmured softly in her ear, and she realized she was making sounds that were just as incoherent, just as meaningless, yet full of meaning.

A moment later, she heard him say something quite distinctly...something about the next dance. She knew at once that he was referring to the dance he'd promised her at the wedding and she laughed weakly, knowing that his euphemism had been very apt, indeed. Surely their whole joyous performance had been choreographed in advance, based on a classic system of body mechanics and techniques perfected over all the centuries since man and woman had been created. A complex, kinetic composition that they had executed with as much grace, harmony and fluency as any ballet.

"Is this the castle in Camelot you described to me?" she murmured, looking up at the soaring ceiling.

He lifted his head and looked at her lovingly, and his smile flashed white in the shadows of his face. "The bed's probably more comfortable than any you'd find in Camelot," he said softly. "I imagine they had to make do with straw pallets or smelly sheepskins." He paused, nodding. "Sometimes real life is better than fantasy."

He sounded so satisfied with himself that she laughed and hugged him close, then stopped laughing as he moved over her again and she felt, incredibly, the start of a new series of explosions along her nervous system. Kissing him gently, delicately, she indicated her wish to take charge this time. So far he had received and acknowledged every signal she'd made to him. This time was no exception. He slid off her onto his side and lay still while she moved her hand over his face, down to his throat, across the firm warmth of shoulder and down over arm and hand to the pulsing strength that was between them.

As her fingers closed gently over him, he inhaled jerkily, then smiled at her as she gently eased him inside her. "Do you suppose Cinderella and the prince ever got around to anything so delightful?" he whispered.

"I wouldn't be at all surprised." She ran her tongue lightly across his chin, loving the clean salty taste of him, and eased herself closer to him, marveling again at how wonderfully well they fitted together.

For a long time they lay very still together, looking into each other's eyes without really seeing each other, their senses straining to enjoy the pleasure of being joined without motion. And then, with a small sigh, Blythe gave in to the impatience he had been so gallantly suppressing, moving her hips suggestively against his, rolling with him until he was above her, smiling down at her as he began the next movements in the dance that had been formalized long before either of them had been born.

Her arousal this time was a slow spiraling warmth that grew to fiery heat as his movements became more impetuous, less studied. Her blood seemed to hum through her body, filling her with an energy to match his. Her eyes were open, watching him, glorying in the dark tense expression of his face, the gleam of his narrowed eyes, the glint of teeth biting down hard on his lower lip as he pulled her with him into a realm of darkness shot through with light, a place of tumbling stars and round mist-circled moons that were really the lights in the hall but seemed now to be transformed into soundlessly whirling planets in the sky of some distant universe.

"So THAT'S HOW IT'S SUPPOSED TO BE," Blythe said drowsily some two hours later.

Michael laughed. "I had pretty much the same thought," he explained when she looked at him questioningly.

She sighed. "No one should ever make love in

anything but a water bed," she said, and Michael hugged her. His skin felt cool to her now, and she reached down to pull the covers up over both of them. "I'm disappointed," she said against his deliciously warm mouth. "I thought you'd have satin sheets. Black satin, maybe."

"Too slippery," he murmured. "You might have slid out from under me."

"Oh? You've tried them, then?"

Laughing, he shook his head and pulled her head down to his shoulder, rocking her against him. The bed felt like a cradle, she decided. Perhaps that was why she felt so guiltless. The innocence of the image made their union seem innocent.

She had only tactile memories of the past couple of hours. Flesh sliding against warm flesh, mouths meeting, parting, hands touching, stroking and gripping, voices murmuring. The other areas of her brain seemed to have slept through it all, leaving imprinted on her retinas only a jumbled collage of dark eyes and hair, a smiling, gently parted mouth, a sudden tender glance. She remembered sleepily that at some time they had taken a shower together. She could vaguely remember playfully massaging the silky dark hair on his chest with soap-smeared hands, laughing like a child. Now she was waking up to the fact that a lot of time had passed. Beyond the soaring, undraped windows the moon hung above the ocean, motionless in an inky black sky, silvering the water.

"I have to go," she murmured reluctantly.

He made a small movement of his head that might have been a nod, but didn't release her from his arms.

"I have to work in the office all day tomorrow. Today."

She felt him smile against her cheek. "I'm glad you aren't driving. I'd hate to entrust those poor tourists to you after such a night."

"I'll be lucky to keep my eyes open all day. And how I'll ever sing tonight...."

He lifted his head and looked at her. "You want to take a short nap? I could wake you at seven and drive you to Chez Michel. We could have a quick breakfast before you pick up your car."

"I'd better go now. I'll have enough explaining to do."

"To Craig?"

"If he's there. David, anyway. I don't know what I'm going to tell Craig."

She felt a sudden plummeting sensation in her stomach. She had betrayed Craig totally. And she did love him—though the past few hours had shown her she didn't love him quite enough or perhaps not in the right way. She'd had no idea she even possessed such a passionate nature. It was probably as well she'd discovered it now. What if she'd discovered it after marriage? She somehow couldn't imagine Craig—

"Are you going to tell him about me?" Michael asked.

She shook her head. "I can't do that. It would... he'd be terribly hurt. He's already jealous. I'll have to tell him that things have changed between him and me, that I can't go on...seeing him as more than a friend. But I don't have to tell him why. I don't think there's any need for him to know about you."

"Why not? Are you afraid he might shoot to kill?"

She laughed, though she felt his voice had reflected disappointment in her. What did he expect?

That she tell everyone of the relationship between them, shout it from the highest hill? "Craig wondered the same about you," she said evenly. "He thought you looked the type who'd carry a knife."

"Only to spread pâté on the thinnest of wafers." His voice was light. "All of you have a pretty poor impression of me, don't you?"

She sighed. "You do have a sort of recklessness about you. Like a pirate."

He sat up, laughing and shaking his head as he ran his fingers through his hair. "Let me see now," he said as he started counting off on his fingers. "Agent 007, a thief, a pirate, some kind of Apache with a knife concealed in his loincloth. Did I miss one?"

"A riverboat gambler."

He looked down at her, smiling fondly. "Blythe, Blythe. The only gambling I've ever done was connected with my pool hustling. And I wasn't very good at that. I don't even bet on jai alai, and everyone bets on jai alai. As for cards, I gave up poker in college when I found I couldn't remember if a flush was better than three of a kind, or vice versa. I never was sure what a full house was until I owned my first restaurant. Plus, my dear love, I have never stolen as much as a hotel ashtray and I always drive the speed limit, unlike James Bond. In fact, I'm the soul of propriety, an upright citizen who pays all his taxes and does only good works."

His face was expressing such self-satisfaction that she couldn't help laughing, even while her mind pondered the words it had seized on. *My dear love.* The endearment meant nothing, of course. The past few hours had been an interlude of wonderful, certainly exciting mating between two consenting and physically healthy adults, nothing more.

He laughed again as they stood on opposite sides of the bed, pulling on their clothes. "You know, Blythe, it's just occurred to me that you are the only woman I've ever made love to who didn't demand first that I tell her I loved her."

It took her a second to suppress the sudden chill that came over her, but when she answered him she was able to produce a voice as light as his own. "And did you tell those other women you loved them?"

"When pressed." He grinned at her. "I did love them at the time. I've always loved women. Probably because I have a pretty terrific mother. I must confess, though, that I've never learned to separate love and sex. It's my one flaw."

This time she couldn't quite manage such a light tone. "Well, I certainly wouldn't want you to love *me*."

He straightened in the act of pulling on a sock, quite obviously startled. "You sound adamant. Should I be insulted again?"

She tied the sash of her jump suit in a tight bow, willing herself not to hesitate. "If you like," she said airily. "I didn't mean it as an insult. But I can't think of a worse fate than being loved by you, unless it was loving you in return."

"What's not to love?" His voice sounded slightly muffled, probably because he was bent over. He'd finished putting on his socks and was sitting on the side of his bed, pushing his feet into his shoes.

For a moment she looked at the back of his dark head and considered hurling a pillow at it. "Didn't we agree that you were a philanderer? And unreliable? And unwilling to make commitments?"

"So we did." He flashed his usual wry smile over his shoulder, stood up and headed for the bedroom door. "I'll go warm up the pumpkin," he said.

The words reminded her of his tendency to fantasize. Obviously he thought of this...interlude as a fantasy. What had it meant to her? She certainly wasn't going to make the usual feminine mistake that he'd referred to so jokingly, that of confusing sex with love, but all the same, she had felt more than mere desire for Michael Channing. Even now, thinking of some of the things that had passed between them, she could feel the heat of passion curling up from low down in her body to suffuse her face with color that would surely match her jump suit.

But she mustn't make the mistake of confusing passion with love, either. True love, to Blythe Sherwood, was sharing of ideals and responsibilities, putting the other person first, working together toward a common goal, understanding each other.

That was the way she'd loved Craig. She could feel the beginnings of sadness that their relationship would have to be different now. Even so, she couldn't regret making love with Michael. She had been unable to resist her own feelings. And that in itself said a lot about what was lacking between her and Craig. Perhaps someday she'd find another sensible man like Craig who could also inspire passion in her.

Michael certainly wasn't the man for her, not on any long-term basis. She could never in a million years understand Michael the way she understood Craig. She wasn't sure Michael knew what the word "responsibility" meant. She had no idea what his ideals were, or if he even had any. Making money? Getting maximum fun out of life?

He had shown her great consideration this night, but hadn't that been designed so that his own enjoyment might be increased?

No, whatever it was she felt for Michael Channing, it wasn't love. So why did she suddenly feel, as she made her way through the house to the open front door and the sound of waves breaking, that she couldn't possibly get through the rest of the day without him? Why did she know with such certainty that she would only be half-alive until she saw him again?

6

BLYTHE COULDN'T BELIEVE her good fortune. When she
let herself into the apartment, she guessed by the
abandoned feel of it that no one was there. A glance
in David's bedroom confirmed her guess, and then
she found a note from him in the kitchen, evidently
written early the previous evening:

> Craig and I are meeting with some people about
> the harbor-cruise deal. We'll probably spend the
> night at his place. Come over for breakfast,
> Craig says. Unless you'd rather sleep late.

Her relief was so overwhelming that she realized
how much she'd been dreading having to explain
her absence. It had never occurred to her to deceive
David by lying about her whereabouts, and she
wasn't going to lie now, but at least she had some
breathing space, some time to prepare her explana-
tions. And time to sleep. A quick glance at her watch
informed her she could get three hours if she went
without breakfast, dropped her jump suit off at the
cleaners on the way to work and waited to shampoo
her hair until after the office closed.

Within seconds she was in bed, feeling the hazy,
tingling warmth that heralded sleep. A corner of her
mind tried to worry her with guilt over missing the
meeting, though she hadn't known it was sched-

uled. Wanderlust was hoping to combine an evening dinner cruise with their Seaport Village tour. From David's note, she decided sleepily, it appeared the plan was about to become reality.

Reality. Reality was waking to the shrill voice of the alarm at eight o'clock with a brain that felt about as alert as cotton candy. She stumbled through her shower, makeup and hair-braiding routine in a zombielike trance, yawning hugely.

It seemed possible that some elements of pleasure might be lurking behind the fog that shrouded her brain, but until she could rest up and get rid of the load of guilt she was carrying around, she couldn't seem to pull the pleasure to the surface.

The drive to her office in the bright sunlight and brisk breeze of a lively Sunday morning helped a little. Along the Embarcadero the tops of the palm trees tossed like feather dusters in the wind. The color of the water in the harbor varied from powder blue to indigo, and the surface rippled, sparkled in the sun. With another four or five hours of sleep, she thought wryly, she might have come halfway alive. Wasn't sex, especially good sex, supposed to make you feel you could climb a mountain? Why, then, did she feel as though the mountain had dropped on her head?

By widening her eyes and tilting her head, she managed to pantomime interest in Craig and David's exuberant account of their successful meeting and then told them that yes, her singing had gone over well again. She even managed not to flinch with guilt when Craig planted an enthusiastic kiss on her cheek and told her she looked terrific—he was glad she'd managed to get a good night's sleep.

She decidedly did *not* look terrific, she admitted to

herself as she glanced in the office mirror after the two men had left, Craig to deliver people to the zoo, David to make the La Jolla run. Only the judicious application of blusher had given her the apparent glow of health.

What she really felt like, she ruefully decided, was an intended victim of the guillotine who'd received a last-minute stay of execution. It was a relief to know she could wait until the next day to tell Craig things had changed between them. They would all be off duty and she'd have had a chance to sleep. She wouldn't have to go anywhere until she reported to Domingo for Monday-evening's short rehearsal.

Somehow she dragged herself through the day. David and Craig insisted on taking her out for pizza to celebrate their new tour. They didn't seem to notice how subdued she was, or how tired. There wasn't time really. She had to excuse herself to pick up her jump suit from the cleaners and get ready to go to the Starlight Room. Halfheartedly she asked them if they'd like to come along, but they refused. They wanted to spend the evening working out the logistics of the dinner cruise and deciding how much to charge for it.

Her head felt no clearer after she arrived at Chez Michel, even though she'd taken a shower and shampooed her hair before coming in. If anything her brain seemed to get thicker and woollier as the evening progressed, but it wasn't until the second break that she realized it wasn't merely fatigue that was numbing her brain, or the new "smokiness" of her voice that was giving her the deep husky sound. "I'm afraid I'm coming down with a cold," she told Michael when he joined her and Domingo at their table.

"You're sure it's not the Cinderella complex?" he murmured, looking at her intently in a way that made her overheated temperature climb another five degrees.

For a moment she thought he was referring to the fairy tale again, but then she realized he was talking about Colette Dowling's best-selling book. *Women's hidden fear of independence,* she mused. He was suggesting the cold might be psychosomatic, self-induced as an excuse not to sing. Which was ridiculous. Domingo had indeed invited her to stay on, and she had agreed without hesitation.

"More likely too many late nights," she objected.

"That does lower one's resistance," he teased, dark eyes glinting with amusement at his own double entendre.

She laughed tiredly. "Or else it's retribution," she said half-seriously as Domingo turned to speak to someone at the next table.

"You don't really believe that, do you?" he demanded. "Don't tell me you're starting to feel guilty? We're friends, Blythe. We didn't do anything hundreds of other couples haven't...."

His voice had risen a little, and Domingo turned around to see what was going on. "Hey," he exclaimed, his gaze fastening on Blythe's face. "You don't look so hot. I mean you do look hot." He leaned across the table, pressed one hand to her forehead and whistled softly. "Home to bed for you, my beauty," he ordered.

"I can finish," she insisted. "I can't be sick. I don't have time to be sick."

"You think you're so indispensable no one can get along without you?"

She nodded, smiling at him with what felt like

watery eyes. "Yeah, well, you're right," he said.
"Which is why you'd better get rested up and skip
rehearsals for a few days until you're better. Okay?"

She didn't feel up to objecting anymore. She was
beginning to feel decidedly feverish. Michael stood
up and took her arm and escorted her to the door.
"I'm sorry, Blythe," he said softly. "I shouldn't have
sounded off like that. I didn't realize you were feeling quite so unwell." He looked at her ruefully. "I
guess I won't see you tonight. I'm sorry about that. I
was looking forward to it."

"I can't come home with you every night, anyway."

He grinned. "Why not?"

"I have work to do," she said wearily.

"Your work is here with me."

She looked at him, suddenly feeling very cold inside, with a deep chill that had nothing to do with
her illness. "Is that why you got me the job here,
Michael, so I'd be available when you want me?"

"Of course," he said cheerfully.

Her shocked reaction must have shown on her
face. He took hold of her shoulders and shook her a
little. "Don't be a goose," he said. "I was only joking."

He did joke a lot, of course. But all the same....
She shook her head, too woozy to think. "I have to
go home," she said faintly.

At once he looked apologetic. "Of course you do.
I've no business keeping you on your feet." He hesitated, looking at her. "I'd better drive you home in
your car. I can take a cab back here to get mine."

She didn't have the strength to object to this
arrangement, though she knew Craig and David
would both be home and might happen to look out

and see him, precipitating an argument she wasn't up to.

Perhaps her cold was psychosomatic, she thought as she hauled herself up the outside steps to the apartment. She surely couldn't be expected to make any confessions and get into any fights as long as she felt this lousy, could she?

HER DOCTOR DIAGNOSED not a cold but influenza. Craig took over, as he'd always done when she or David was sick. He insisted on taking her temperature morning and evening, questioning her every time he came in to make sure she followed the program of bedrest, decongestants and lots of liquids the doctor had recommended. "You sound like a TV commercial," she joked weakly.

Nevertheless she was grateful for his ministrations. Though he and David were gone during the day, he checked on her by telephone when he could, popped in between tours to make sure she had a pitcher of iced Gatorade and plenty of tissues handy. In the evenings he made her tea sweetened with honey, fed her spoonfuls of cough medicine, plumped her pillows and placed soothingly warm damp cloths across her aching eyes.

She felt increasingly guilty, but she just couldn't tell him, not until she regained her strength.

Adding to her guilt was the fact that Michael also called every day and sent over chicken soup he'd had one of his chefs make, flowers with cards signed by Temptation and the staff of Chez Michel and a bright-pink, heart-shaped Mylar balloon, on which he'd scrawled in purple ink, "I miss you." The gift made her smile. Naturally Michael Channing wouldn't send roses like any traditional lover. All the same, though recognizing she was a coward, she hid the balloon under her bed. But she couldn't hide her conscience. Whenever Craig was in the room, she could sense the balloon glowing in the dark under there and felt uncomfortable, amazed that he didn't seem to feel its presence.

Michael wanted to come to visit her, but she made him see how impossible that was as long as Craig still believed his status was unaltered. "I can't tell him now," she croaked into the telephone receiver. "He'll just put it down to delirium and refuse to accept it."

Michael told her he understood, but she still felt like a coward. She also felt oddly disoriented, which she blamed on the decongestants. And empty, which was probably due to the limbo she'd had to put her emotions in.

By Thursday, the combination of megavitamins, drugs and chicken soup had taken hold, and she was able to tell Michael when he telephoned in the early afternoon that her health was improving, though she doubted she'd be able to sing that weekend... her voice was still inclined to sound gravelly. "Julie took over the office for the week," she told him. "We're planning on hiring a new person in a month or two, but Julie's offered to help out for a while. She gave up her volunteer work when she married Russ, but she found sitting in the house all day didn't suit her at all."

"That was quite a long speech," Michael said warmly when she stopped for breath. "You must be feeling better. Are you kissable yet?"

"Don't you dare come up here," she said at once. "I still haven't had a chance to say anything to Craig and...."

"Surely there's no reason your concerned employer can't come to check on you now that your health is improving?"

"Michael—" She stopped for a sneeze and inadvertently caught sight of her red-rimmed eyes, swollen nose and lank hair in the metal cover of the Kleenex box by her bed. "Please don't come here. I don't want you to see me, and I have to get over this before—"

"Okay," he said cheerfully, and hung up.

An hour later she was awakened from a doze by the sound of the doorbell. "Oh, no," she muttered, pulling her tailored navy robe from the bedside chair. "He wouldn't. He couldn't."

Opening the door, she determinedly straightened her spine, hoping posture alone would give her voice the conviction it needed to insist Michael couldn't come in. But to her surprise there was no one there. About to close the door, wondering if she had imagined the ringing bell, she noticed a package lying on the wooden veranda outside the door. It was a fairly large cardboard box, but it felt quite light when she picked it up and took it in.

Whoever had sealed the box had done a thorough job of it, and after pulling at the wrappings for a while, she had to finally go in the kitchen and get a knife to cut the tape.

The wrappings fell away to disclose a large, stuffed, virulently green frog made of velvet. It had absurdly long legs and enormous webbed feet. A silver foil crown sat rakishly on its head.

Laughing, she held the frog up so that she could examine its whimsically smiling face. "Michael Channing, you are a devil," she said aloud.

There was a card tied on a string around the frog's neck. "Kiss me and your dreams will come true."

Without hesitation, still laughing, she did as instructed. Immediately the doorbell rang again. Looking out through the kitchen window, she saw Michael looking in at her, hands cupped around his face, nose pressed against the glass. He was grinning wickedly. Her heart leaped, not from the shock of seeing him so unexpectedly but from sheer pleasure at the sight of him.

Quite suddenly she understood that the odd emptiness she'd felt over the past several days was acute loneliness. She'd missed Michael Channing as much as she might have missed part of her own body. The past few days had been an arid desert without light or life. She felt a sudden yearning to be in his arms, to hear his voice telling her ... telling her what? *That he loved her.* That's what she wanted him to tell her, in spite of all her protestations to him and to herself, in spite of her much vaunted wisdom in recognizing that he was the "love-'em-and-leave-'em" type. She wanted to be reassured, as though she were a child. Because *she* loved *him*—desperately, consumingly.

Afraid to pause to consider this sudden insight, she drew in a deep breath, composed her features into a bright smile and hurried to open the door, still holding the frog. "You are an absolute idiot," she said, and was as taken aback as he by the trembling note in her voice.

For a second they looked at each other in a startled way. "Blythe?" he said. Abruptly there was uncertainty in his smile.

A moment's strained silence and he recovered his usual poise. "Is that any way to address a prince?" he asked.

Whatever her answer might have been, she was never to find out. Without knowing she was going to do so, she reached out one hand toward him in a helpless little gesture. He immediately stepped into the apartment, closed the door behind him and pulled her into his arms. "You're still not feeling well, are you?" he said softly.

Her face safely hidden against his suit jacket, Blythe closed her eyes in relief that he'd interpreted her tremulous behavior in such a way. If he even suspected how important he had become to her he would head for the nearest exit. She might not always understand him, but she knew him well enough to make that particular prediction.

She allowed herself one more brief moment of clinging to him. Then she straightened and said briskly, "It's not every day a girl turns a toad into a prince. I guess my success went to my head."

Lifting her chin with one long finger, he studied her face for a moment, then allowed his narrowed eyes to widen in an outraged expression. "A toad! I'll have you know this is the finest of frogs—*Rana catesbeiana*—eighteen inches from his snout to the tip of his toes, just like his real-life counterpart." Tilting his head back, he gave her a steamy glance from under hooded eyelids. "You do realize that now that you've brought your prince to life you're responsible for his happiness?"

Her tremulousness had receded under the force of his playfulness. She felt content to be happy that he was there. "I'm ready to serve, as always," she said lightly, and was prepared when he lowered his head to kiss her.

But not prepared for the yearning response that swept through her. Yes, she loved him. And she didn't want to think about the heartbreak that was eventually going to be hers.

His kiss was deeper, more sensual than ever. Though perhaps her imagination was reading more into his technique because she wanted to read more into it. All the same, it was a wonderful kiss that seemed to gather together all the loneliness, all the discomfort, all the worries of the past few days and send them winging into the air as if they had never existed.

After a while he reached to lift her in his arms and carry her into the bedroom, where he sat her down on the edge of the bed. "Michael," she protested breathlessly, though she knew if he wanted to make love to her she wasn't going to have the strength to refuse him.

He kissed her forehead lightly, pulled a couple of pillows into place in front of the padded headboard and pushed her back against them. "Don't worry," he said cheerfully. "I'm not cad enough to take advantage of a sick woman, even if she does look adorable with a red nose. Do you happen to have a relative named Rudolph by any chance?"

As he spoke, he was smoothing the sheet and blanket into place around her, settling the pillows behind her. "I do look awful, don't I?" she moaned.

He sat down on the edge of the bed, cupped her face in his hands and dropped a kiss on the object of his teasing. "A red nose has never looked as beautiful," he proclaimed. "You'd better not go outside, or you'll start a whole new fashion. For miles around, young women will be painting their noses with blusher, trying to emulate the latest punk fad set by Blythe Sherwood, the famous pop singer."

His mischievously smiling face was barely an inch from her own. She could feel his breath on her skin, warm and clean. Close up, his odd assortment of features seemed even more asymmetrical than usual. The fingers of her right hand reached to trace the laugh lines at the corner of his left eye, then slid down to the comma shape that bracketed one side of his mouth. She remembered suddenly that she'd thought he might be an actor when she first met him. A movie actor, she thought now, romantic movies only. In close-up, the slow intent gaze of his dark eyes was as hypnotic as any on the silver screen. "Rudolph Valentino," she murmured.

He grinned. "Not that Rudolph. Santa's Rudolph."

Her hand slipped to his mouth and he kissed her fingers delicately, then removed them and touched his mouth to her lips. "Germs," she whispered.

"Princes are immune to such common organisms." His mouth closed over hers before she could protest again, and she felt herself sliding once more into the honeyed pleasure of sweet passion, her arms closing around his shoulders as he lifted her to him. So slowly, so gently, his mouth moved against hers, silken in its deliberate restraint. His hands tightened around her, burning through the thin wool of her robe as they slid softly over her breasts. She knew that at any moment he was going to throw restraint aside, and she didn't have any real intention of stopping him.

His mouth was moving downward now, sliding over her throat to the place where her robe lapels overlapped. Gently he removed one hand from her body to untie the robe's sash, letting the garment fall open. He smiled over the sensible flannelette of her gown and made a lazy, drawn-out game of untying the ribbons that held it closed. She watched his face as he gazed at her bared breasts, admiring the clean outline of his jaw, the dark-lashed eyelids half-lowered over the gleaming eyes. "You are so perfectly made," he murmured. "Like a statue created by an artist in love with his model."

"Too skinny," she whispered.

"Slender," he corrected.

He raised his eyes to hers. "Blythe?" he questioned, and she felt her breath catch in her throat.

"Yes," she said.

It did occur to her at one point to wonder what would happen if David decided to check on her. It wasn't likely. Craig had gone on the Tijuana run today, and David had his hands full with zoo trips and assisting Julie in the office. In any case, she apparently wasn't capable of worrying about interruptions, not when Michael was holding her close against his warm, now naked body.

She could only remember vaguely when he'd removed his clothes. His lips hadn't left hers for a moment, not until he'd gently pulled her nightgown over her head. Then he'd held her for a long time, not speaking, his mouth brushing hers once in a while with unimaginable tenderness. She liked being held, she'd discovered. Craig had never had much patience with preliminaries, not after the first time or two. He'd prided himself on being a straightforward lover, and she hadn't known that straightforwardness wasn't always the most enjoyable. She had suspected, though, that their relationship was more like that of a couple who had been married for twenty years.

She squirmed a little in Michael's arms. What was she doing? What kind of woman compared lovers in this way?

Michael mistook her squirming for impatience, and he began the slow stroking that always aroused her to a pitch of excitement she would not have believed possible in her pre-Michael days. When he entered her, she was ready for him, and she moved with him without thought, her mind empty of everything but sensation.

Michael seemed to know exactly when to move, when to pause, when to hold her tightly, when to set her free to lift and arch her body in its own paroxysms of delight. And she in turn seemed to have a knowledge she'd never possessed before, or suspected she possessed. She could tell by his breathing when his excitement was rising, tell by the measured thrusts of his body that he was getting ready to ride the crest of his own passion. And she knew instinctively when the moment had come to simply hold on to him and soar with him to an ultimate shuddering climax.

They lay still together afterward for what seemed a long time, but might only have been minutes. Then he leaned over her and kissed her gently. She thought perhaps the whole spiral of lovemaking was about to begin again and, incredibly, felt an aching within that heralded the beginning of renewed desire. But even as her lips warmed to his and increased their pressure, he pulled himself away from her, looked at her ruefully and said, "I guess I am enough of a cad to take advantage of a sick woman, after all."

Giving a dramatically audible sigh, he stood up and headed for the bathroom. Moments later he reappeared and began dressing.

Feeling remarkably restored, Blythe went to the

bathroom herself, then pulled on her flannelette gown, frowning at Michael when he smirked. "It's comfortable," she said defensively.

He nodded. "And sexy."

"Hardly."

His eyes gleamed with amusement. "It must be. Something transported me into Camelot."

Camelot. City of legend. Romantic heroes fighting with lances for fair ladies. For Camelot she had given up her established dream of a good, comfortable, secure marriage. For Camelot she had jeopardized the wonderful three-way relationship she and Craig and David had enjoyed for so long. Was it worth it? She sighed. Yes, it was worth it. Michael was worth it. All the same, somewhere in her chest an ache began that had nothing to do with her illness.

Michael finished dressing right after Blythe climbed back into bed. After a final settling of the knot in his tie, he leaned over her and touched his fingers to her cheek. "Take care of yourself for me," he said softly, then added, "I'd take care of you myself if the circumstances permitted. You know that, don't you?"

The tenderness in his voice made her heart skip several beats, though she doubted he would take care of her as Craig had. Michael was much more suited to party atmospheres and brightly lit restaurants than the drab responsibilities of the sickroom. But she nodded, and he grinned in his usual devilish manner and started to turn away. She felt a return of the aching emptiness at the thought of his leaving. She wanted to beg him to stay, to continue holding her, to never let her go. And that would be the worst possible way to treat someone like him. With a soft sound of distress, she closed her eyes against the wave of despair that suddenly washed over her.

At once he sat down beside her again. "Blythe, are you all right? Can I get you anything?"

"I'm just sleepy, I guess," she lied. She was afraid to open her eyes in case he would see how much she wanted him to stay.

His lips touched her forehead once more. "I probably shouldn't have come to see you," he murmured. "It was very selfish of me, but I was missing my good friend."

His good friend. Another wave of despair washed over her. She kept her eyes firmly closed and felt him tucking the covers around her again, fussing with them until they apparently satisfied him. A moment later she heard the outer door close.

She opened her eyes and saw he'd tucked the frog in beside her. Laughing weakly, not wanting to admit even to herself that she felt more like bursting into tears, she hugged the idiotic animal close. "Oh, Michael," she murmured helplessly, then closed her eyes again and willed herself to sleep so that she wouldn't have to think.

SHE AWOKE THIS TIME to the sounds of kitchen activity and the wonderful smell of chili con carne...David's specialty. She realized that for the first time in days, she felt ravenously hungry. "Hey, can I have some of that?" she called out groggily.

To her dismay, Craig's smiling face appeared around the doorjamb. "You were asleep when David looked in earlier," he told her, then added in the same breath, "What the hell is that?"

He was staring at a spot just left of her shoulder.

Uncomprehendingly Blythe followed the direction of his gaze and saw to her horror that the frog was protruding from the bedcovers. He had somehow lost his crown. His head was tilted at an angle that looked quizzical. She swallowed against the sudden dryness in her throat. "It's a frog," she said lamely.

"Well, I can see that much." Craig had crossed the room as he spoke, and now he picked up the frog before she could clear her mind enough to grab hold of it. He was smiling. "That's the craziest animal I've ever seen," he said. "It looks like Kermit. Look at those feet. Where on earth did it come from? Julie?"

She was almost weak enough to seize on the possible explanation, but even as the thought went through her mind and was dismissed as cowardice, Craig discovered the card and read it. His gray eyes met hers, and they were suddenly as bleak as a rainwashed sky. "Michael Channing," he said with absolute certainty.

Blythe nodded, letting out her breath with a sigh.

"He was here? Today?"

She nodded again.

"For how long?"

"A couple of hours or so."

"Why?"

Her heart was beating like a hammer on wood. Like a judge's gavel. She could see the accusation in Craig's eyes, read the verdict that was forming in his mind. *Guilty, your honor.* "He is, more or less, my employer," she pointed out, then squirmed inwardly at her cowardice. Taking a deep breath, she sat up straight and faced Craig directly. "He was concerned about me. He came to cheer me up."

Craig glanced at the card, his lips curling. "To make your dreams come true?"

"It's a joke between us," she explained. "Michael has this thing about fairy tales and fantasy."

"Are you having an affair with Channing?"

She felt a piercing sensation. How sordid that sounded. She couldn't confess to it, couldn't bring herself to tell him.

Before she could decide how to answer, Craig flung the frog onto a chair and glared at her. "Was that why he came here? To make love to you, here in this apartment, where you wouldn't ever—"

"Craig," she protested. Even though she could not avoid hurting him, she could at least spare him every detail.

"Michael stayed a couple of hours," she repeated wearily. "He brought the frog and we...talked and then he left." She forced herself to look directly at Craig.

Incredibly he was smiling. Abruptly he sat down on the edge of the bed and pulled her into his arms. "Well, I'm glad to hear things haven't gone as far as I suspected." He rested his cheek against hers. "You've no idea how my imagination was running away with me," he added softly.

David chose that moment to poke his head around the door. He had a wooden spoon in his hand and a large, gaudily striped apron over his T-shirt and jeans. "Do you guys want sour cream or cheese on your chili?" he asked. Seeing them together on the bed, he raised his light eyebrows in an exaggerated way until they nearly disappeared under the curly blond hair that had tumbled over his forehead during his kitchen duty. "Excuse *me*!" he said loudly, and withdrew his head with alacrity. "Sour cream *and* cheese," he muttered, apparently to himself.

"Craig, please," Blythe said softly. "I'm not...I

can't, there's something I have to tell you. I've wanted to tell you, meant to tell you, that I've stopped feeling the way I used to about you, but then I got sick and I just couldn't.... My feelings for you aren't what they were. I'm really not sure how I feel about you. I'm confused, I guess. I do care about you, Craig. You must know that. But—"

His expression had hardened as she spoke. "We've always said one day we'd be married," he said harshly. He took a deep breath and shook his head, then touched her cheek lightly, his expression softening. "I guess we've put it off long enough, haven't we? Maybe we should set a date, make it official, buy a ring...."

Panicked, she raised a hand to ward him off as he leaned closer. "No, Craig, please, you don't understand."

He pulled back, looking earnestly into her face. "I know I'm not one for romantic gestures and sweet talk and all that, but you always said you liked me that way. Remember the story you read in *Good Housekeeping*? The one about the woman who was married to the practical man? She envied her neighbor because her husband was so romantic? And then her neighbor said, 'Yes, but it never occurs to him to carry out the garbage.' Remember that? You told me right then that romance wasn't important to you."

"I guess I was wrong," she said gently, troubled by the pleading expression on his face.

"Then I'll change. I'll buy you roses and heart-shaped boxes of candy and—"

"Oh, Craig." She pulled him close and held him for a moment, feeling as though she'd committed the greatest sin in the universe. "It wouldn't make any difference," she murmured. "You must know there isn't enough between us to make a marriage work. We never seriously talked about marriage, anyway—it was just a joking thing. Don't you see, you and I just sort of drifted into a relationship. We never did have a great flaring passion between us."

He straightened and looked at her with suddenly narrowed eyes. "Are you telling me that's what you have with Michael Channing?"

She sighed. "I'm not talking about Michael, Craig."

"You're in love with each other? He's told you he's in love with you?"

"No. I don't—"

"Because if you believe that, you'll believe anything. I told you, Michael Channing changes women as often as some men change their underwear. He's just amusing himself with you. He told everyone after his divorce that he was never going to let a woman affect his emotions again. Julie told me he really idolized his wife. But still, he just walked out on her one day for no reason. Julie said she was devastated, couldn't understand why he left her."

She felt a sinking sensation. Michael had refused to tell her what had happened to his marriage. If only she knew, she could defend him. But she didn't know. "You've discussed him with Russ and Julie? When? And why?"

He moved uncomfortably on the bed, making the springs creak a little. "A few days ago. After Russ and Julie came back from Puerto Vallarta. You were getting so involved with him, with the singing and everything, I was worried." Anger abruptly replaced his sheepish expression. "I should never have let you take that job with Domingo. I knew it would lead to something with Michael Channing."

She sighed. "The singing doesn't have anything to do with this."

"Are you sure? Which came first, Blythe, the singing or the seduction? He heard you sing at the wedding, right? He wanted you to sing at his restaurant. How do you know he didn't make...advances to you so you'd agree to take the job? Every other woman he's had since his divorce hasn't lasted longer than a week. Maybe his interest in you stems from the fact that you turned out to be a drawing card. He wants to keep you happy so you'll stay with it."

"That's ridiculous!"

He stood up, looking down at her with a grim smile. "You think about it. See if I'm not right. Better yet, give up the singing and see how Michael Channing treats you then." His face softened all of a sudden, and he reached down to touch her cheek gently, tenderly. "Look, you're really not up to this. We'll talk about it when you feel better." He smiled suddenly, and even though Blythe felt terrible about what she was putting him through, there was something about that smile that made her angry. It looked...patronizing. "We don't even have to talk about it, then," he added briskly. "I'm perfectly willing to forget this conversation ever took place. I can overlook this whole thing if you'll promise me you won't see Channing again."

"I'm not going to promise any such thing," she said wearily. "And it wouldn't make any difference, anyway, Craig. I'm—"

His fingers touched her lips to silence. "We won't talk about it anymore. As soon as you come to your senses, let me know. We've known each other a long time, Blythe. I'll always be here, waiting."

With another warm smile he turned toward the door, adding over his shoulder, "I'll bring your chili in now."

About to tell him she felt well enough to eat in the kitchen, Blythe bit back the words. She just wasn't up to facing Craig and David together. She could hear Craig's voice murmuring in the kitchen now, probably telling David nothing was wrong, they'd just had a minor spat and she would be over it by morning.

She sighed and leaned back against the pillows, suddenly feeling weary again. Maybe she should have told Craig she was desperately in love with Michael Channing. Should she call him back and tell him now? No. She couldn't do it. She had to let some time go by, let him get used to the fact that she didn't love *him*, at least not in the way a prospective wife should. Poor Craig. Somehow she hadn't expected him to react quite so strongly. He'd never seemed too... passionate about her. How naive she had been. She certainly hadn't expected him to offer to wait for her. He'd do it, too. He was noted for his patience. He'd keep himself in the background, doing small services for her, making her feel guiltier and guiltier.

Yet how dared he suggest that Michael had used her, had deliberately intrigued her and charmed her until she was under his spell, just so she'd perform in the Starlight Room. It was an insult not only to Michael but to her. Craig obviously couldn't conceive of another man being attracted to her for her own sake. It was a particularly poisonous suggestion because there was no way she could combat it, no way she could prove it wasn't so.

Unless....

No. She'd always prided herself on honesty in her relationships, even though she'd slipped a little in the past weeks. She couldn't deliberately set out to find out if there was any truth in Craig's accusation. She couldn't tell Michael she wasn't going to sing anymore and stick to it, then wait to see if he still wanted to be involved with her. She couldn't possibly do anything so underhanded.

There was a cumulative effect from some poisons, she conceded a little later, when both David and Craig, solicitous to a fault, had left her to rest comfortably for the remainder of the night. Arsenic, for example, when ingested in small amounts, could build up gradually, undetected by anyone, until it suddenly reached a large enough quantity to kill. So it was with the poisonous thought Craig had introduced into her mind. First she remembered that Michael had mentioned her singing as one of the things about her that had attracted him. And then when she thought back to the way he had persisted in his pursuit of her, she recalled that soon after she'd started singing at the Starlight Room, he'd disappeared from her life for a while. When her two weeks of trial had almost reached an end, he'd shown up again. Why? In order to persuade her to stay on? No, he'd made love to her *after* she'd agreed.

About to slump back against the pillows with relief, she tensed as another thought came forward from some far-off corner of her mind and presented itself to her. Had he made love to her because she'd done what he wanted? As some kind of reward? Had she been manipulated again?

7

IN THE MORNING, David brought her breakfast on a tray—scrambled eggs, toast, coffee. "I'm not sure I'm hungry," she told him apologetically.

He nodded. "Eat what you can. You need to get your strength back." He hesitated, worrying his curly blond hair with his fingers as he did when he had something on his mind. His lanky body looked unusually tense. She felt a tremor of foreboding. "I hear you and Craig are having troubles," he said slowly.

She nodded, feeling miserable and guilty. "Craig and I just didn't have enough going for us to—"

"I'm not in any hurry to get married myself," David interrupted. "But I made up my mind years ago that I'd marry someone who'd fit in—with the business, I mean. I've always thought it would end up with you and Craig and me and whoever all working together, all family."

She looked up at him, balancing the tray on her knees but feeling even less hungry than before. "I guess I thought that, too," she said gently. "I guess we both needed the security of something like that after mom and dad...." She took a deep breath. "I'm sorry, David. But the fact that Craig and I aren't going to...well, the change needn't interfere with our plans. Craig's not thinking of backing out of the business, is he?"

"No. But you are, aren't you?"

She stared up at him, surprised by the condemning note in his voice. "What makes you say that?"

"Craig says you will if you get any more involved with Michael Channing. You won't have time for the business. Channing's certainly not going to want to get into it. He's got enough on his plate without bothering with a small enterprise like ours."

She swallowed. "You don't like Michael, do you?" she asked pointedly.

"I like him well enough. I even admire him in some ways. He's got a lot of... flair. But I think Craig's right. I think he's turned your head, made you forget about the people who really love you. I think you should stop seeing him."

She looked blankly at the slowly congealing eggs in front of her. *Turned her head.* As though she were a child without any sense of her own. But, then, Craig always had treated her as a child. Not his fault. She'd let him. "I care about Michael, Dave," she said weakly. "I can't just... stop."

He took the tray from her and set it aside, then sat down on the bed and looked at her with astonishment. "Are you saying you're in love with him?"

In the face of his disbelief, she backed down once more. "I'm not sure, Dave. How can anyone be sure?"

"How does he feel? Does he...?" He made a face. "I guess it's none of my business."

She managed to smile up at him. "Everything to do with me is your business, David. But I can't answer your question." She laughed shortly. "As far as I know, he thinks of me as his good friend. Nothing more."

"I don't think Michael Channing's right for you, Blythe."

She laughed tiredly. "I'm inclined to agree with you. But I can't seem to resist the man."

"You don't think you might just be feeling grateful because he got you this chance to sing?"

"Not you, too," she said, sighing. She shook her head. "Maybe it's tied in with the singing. I don't know." She looked up at him. "Craig thinks I should give up on the singing and find out how I feel then."

He nodded solemnly. "That might be the best way."

She stared at him, feeling helpless. What she had wanted, of course, was for him to argue with her, to tell her that she definitely shouldn't give up singing. Instead, he'd made it sound so simple. Didn't he understand what singing had come to mean to her? He was her twin... if he didn't understand, how could she expect anyone else to?

He was studying her intently, looking worried. "I think you've let it get away from you, don't you? I've always enjoyed my guitar, but it's just a hobby. I've never wanted to get seriously involved in it." He laughed. "Who am I kidding? I can strum pretty well, but I'm no Domingo. Nor do I want to be." He hugged her and stood up, looking down at her with sympathy. "I don't want to try to influence you, Blythe, but maybe you should consider giving up singing with Domingo, anyway. He's pretty demanding. All those rehearsals."

"I'll think about it," she said tiredly, and he grinned and handed her the cup of coffee from the tray and carried the rest of the dishes out.

A moment later she heard him on the telephone in the next room, talking to Craig. "She's still not completely well, but she's getting over it, I think. Another couple of days and...." His voice lowered and she couldn't hear the next sentence, and then he said, "Well, I think you're probably right. She needs a little space. Yeah. I'll see you at the office in a few minutes."

She finished the coffee and set the cup down on her bedside table. She had the distinct impression David and Craig had convinced themselves that her feelings for Michael were linked to her cold. They were going to treat her kindly and wait until she showed signs that she was "getting over it."

Maybe they were right. Maybe she would recover from the cold and love at the same time. Could someone recover from love? Michael evidently had. He must have loved his wife once, but she could still hear his cool voice saying that he didn't love her now. She suddenly felt confused and lonely. She didn't know what she would do.

After a while she looked up at the ceiling and nodded silently to herself. Somehow subconsciously a decision had been made for her again. She was going to give up singing for the time being, not particularly to test Michael—though something in her wanted to do that—but so that she could eliminate some of the confusion in her thoughts. Maybe later on she could audition somewhere else, somewhere unconnected with Michael....

MICHAEL CALLED AGAIN THAT DAY, and on Saturday and Sunday, too, but he didn't suggest coming over. He asked on Sunday afternoon if she'd talked to Craig and she said she had, then hesitated. "I didn't exactly tell him everything," she admitted.

"Why not?"

She sighed deeply. Men always seemed to think things could be handled in a totally straightforward manner. Didn't they ever concern themselves with people's feelings? "I didn't want to hurt him," she said weakly.

There was a silence. Then he said softly, "Daisy?"

"Maybe so."

"I don't like the idea of deceiving him," Michael said uneasily. He paused. "I guess I'll have to leave it up to you. But I think you should tell him the truth. It isn't fair to leave him thinking you might go back to him."

She didn't answer, couldn't answer.

After a moment he asked softly, "You're not considering going back to him, are you?"

"Of course not," she said immediately, with more vehemence than she'd intended.

Another silence, then to her relief he changed the subject. "Are you well enough for rehearsal tomorrow? Something's come up and Domingo wants to reschedule for ten in the morning. He's got a lot of stuff he wants to go through with you."

She hesitated, but she couldn't tell him her decision on the telephone. She had to tell him face-to-face, see his expression so she could judge his reaction. She felt a return of the emptiness that had plagued her all week. She didn't want to give up singing. She didn't want to take a chance on losing Michael so soon. And she still felt guilty about Craig. She felt as a hermit crab must feel when it discarded the shell it had been living in...raw and vulnerable.

"I can make it," she said finally.

"I'll tell Domingo." His voice was brisk. "How about lunch afterward? I have to go to Michael's On The Pier. Near Seaport Village."

"Yes, okay." She tried to put some enthusiasm in her voice, but it came out flat.

"Blythe? Is anything wrong?" He was sensitive to her moods, this man. Impossible to deceive.

"I'll see you tomorrow," she said.

After she hung up the telephone, she looked blankly around the living room. She'd started to feel much better the previous day and had dressed and even managed a little housework. She'd pulled the Mylar balloon out from under her bed and found it deflated, limp, the words on it undecipherable. Why did that suddenly seem so symbolic?

She sighed. There wasn't much for her to do today. She'd thought she might go into the office, but Craig had talked her out of it. Julie was managing fine, he'd assured her. As far as Blythe could detect, his manner was as it had always been, affectionate and caring.

Domingo called early on Sunday evening and she assured him she'd be fit enough for rehearsal the next day. He seemed relieved, even excited. He talked for a long time about some new arrangements he and "the boys" had been working on, even talked about the weather, garrulously, as though he didn't want to get off the phone. Amused, Blythe let him ramble on, pricking up her ears when he said Michael had brought Mrs. Berenstein back to the club the previous evening. Michael hadn't mentioned that little detail, she thought, her lips tightening. Domingo seemed to think she would find the news significant, which she certainly did, but she refused to act like a jealous woman. There was no reason Michael should tell her everything he was doing. There was no commitment between them. No commitment at all.

ON MONDAY MORNING Domingo greeted her with open arms and a whole stream of Tagalog. Whenever he got particularly excited he reverted to his native tongue. Hugging her, he swung her around, then set her down and stood beaming at her, looking like a skinny teenager in his T-shirt and blue jeans, rather than a twenty-five-year-old man who was a skilled professional. "Man, have I got news for you!" he exclaimed.

"What? Has something happened?"

"You might say that." He glanced at Stacey and Eddie, who were up on the stage, smiling down at her.

"Okay, tell me, then." She wasn't sure if it was a good thing he was in such a happy mood or not. He was probably going to be pretty mad at her. She'd already let him down over the weekend, even if it wasn't her fault. He was obviously relieved she'd turned up today, and when she told him....

He was still grinning, but his mouth had turned down in a secretive way. "I can't tell you," he said. "I promised Michael I'd let him be the one to give you the word."

"It's something to do with the group?"

He nodded, then set his mouth in a straight line and gestured dramatically across it with one finger. "My lips are zipped."

"I'm having lunch with Michael. Is he going to tell me then?"

Another nod.

"Couldn't you give me a hint?"

A theatrical shake of the black ringlets.

"Maybe you *should* tell me," she urged. "I ... well, I have something to tell you myself."

"It can't be as important as our news. It'll have to wait, anyway. You've been goofing off all week. It's time to go to work."

In the end it seemed easier to go along with him, to climb up on the stage and prepare to work. One last time wouldn't hurt, anyway, she told herself. Afterward she could explain to Michael.

The rehearsal went well, too well. Blythe felt herself being drawn back to the soaring sensation she'd felt before, as though she were letting her real self live. Every time she sang, something seemed to be released inside her. She felt...right. Happy.

At the end of rehearsal, Domingo told her he wanted her to join them at his house during the week to go over some of their own material, maybe make some suggestions about a couple of new songs they were working on. Ever since she'd met him, she'd wanted to get in on the group's songwriting. She had a few ideas herself that.... But that would take up a lot of her time. She'd be letting Craig and David down even more. "I don't know, Domingo," she said miserably. "I'm going to be pretty busy and—"

"See how you feel after you've talked to Michael," he said. "When he tells you...well, you'll see why this has to come first. We have to decide—" He broke off and looked mysterious again. "We'll talk later," he said.

When Michael came in she was sitting at a table with Domingo, going over a song they were having trouble with. She felt the usual rush of pleasure at the sight of him, coupled with the new sensation of yearning that she seemed to be stuck with. Conscious of the group's presence, she had to forcibly stop herself from jumping to her feet and holding out her hands to him. Instead she stood up and smiled and said, "Hello, Michael," as though he were just a casual acquaintance she was reasonably glad to see.

He had no such compunctions. He strode toward her, cupped her face with both his strong, long-fingered hands and studied it intently. "All recovered?" he asked. "You look wonderful, like a daffodil."

Wanting to look cheerful even if she didn't feel it, she had dressed that morning in a tightly belted shirt of canary cotton, worn over green linen pants, and had brushed her hair into shining shoulder-length waves. "Is that better than a lollipop?" she asked.

Michael laughed and pulled her into his arms, kissing her exuberantly. Her arms went automatically around him, and she returned the kiss just as eagerly.

Behind her Domingo murmured, "Ho, ho, ho," and up on the stage Eddie sounded out a long, suggestive roll on his snare drum, ending with a deafening crash of cymbals.

Stacey was smiling broadly. "Well, she did say she was going to be pretty busy," he called down to Domingo.

Michael looked over her shoulder. "Is she all through for now?" he asked.

Domingo laughed. "Looks to me like you'd better get her out of here. You tell her our news, she might get even more friendly, and I don't allow no goings-on in here, man."

"What is this great news everybody's so secretive about?" Blythe asked.

"Later," Michael said. "I'm going to prolong the suspense so you can enjoy it more."

"Michael...." She hesitated, then sighed. "I've something to tell all of you, too," she blurted out. "I'm not going to be able to sing with the group anymore."

His whole body stilled, and he released her abruptly. "You're not what?"

She repeated it, then added, "I feel I should concentrate on Wanderlust for a while. I've really let Craig and David down, and I have to make it up to them."

Behind her there was a moment's deafening silence. Then all three of the group started talking at once. Domingo's voice dominated. "Man, you can't let her do that, not now. Tell her, Michael. Tell her she can't do this to us."

"I'm sorry, Domingo," Blythe began, turning, "but my mind's made up. I've got some problems I have to work through and—"

Michael gripped her arm suddenly, and urged her toward the door. "Let's go," he said.

She glanced up at his face, caught a glimpse of narrowed eyes, a tightly compressed mouth. Over his shoulder he called back to the others. "Don't worry about it. She's not quitting. I'm not going to let her." There was steely determination in his voice.

"Good luck, boss-man," Domingo called.

In the car Michael sat tensely forward over the steering wheel for a moment. Then he looked at her directly, sighed and ran one hand through his hair. "Okay, Daisy. Which are you having second thoughts about, the singing or me?"

She had no idea how to answer him, and after a moment he leaned over to her and kissed her lightly on the mouth. As before his touch stirred her deeply, and without even thinking about her response, she returned the pressure of his lips and let herself lean into the curve of his arms. His hold tightened immediately, and all her worries and concerns seemed to drop away. A mouth that kissed like this could not belong to anyone but a man who cared.

As always he was as intent on giving pleasure as on taking it. His mouth was gentle and tender, butterfly soft against hers, barely touching as he tasted the warmth of her lips with his tongue. "It's not me you're afraid of, then," he said softly after a while. "So I guess it must be the singing."

She started to speak, but he silenced her with a touch of his fingers on her mouth, then moved away from her with obvious reluctance. "Let's eat first," he said. "Things always seem better on a full stomach. After you taste my chef's clam chowder you'll be putty in my hands."

He started the car and began talking about his restaurant on the pier, which she had never visited, though she knew of its reputation for delectable seafood. Evidently the chef he'd mentioned was inclined to be temperamental, and Michael's main purpose in going there today was to calm him down after his latest crisis...a *sous-chef* who had accidentally cooked french fries in oil that had already been used for fish. Alexander, the chef, was insisting the *sous-chef* be fired. Michael was hoping to help the manager change Alexander's mind.

The drive was a short one. And as soon as they arrived at the outdoor restaurant, Michael excused himself for a few minutes. Blythe sat at one of the round tables in the shade of its huge blue umbrella, looking out at the water and the gulls wheeling above the seawall, pondering his reaction to her announcement. *I won't let her quit.* Did he intend just ignoring her wishes? Did he think he could just dismiss her other responsibilities and they would go away?

When he returned, he'd removed his suit jacket and tie and opened the collar of his pale-blue shirt, rolling the sleeves to the elbows. The casual clothing reminded her of how he had looked reflected in the window of his house, and she felt weak inside at the memory. He grinned at her wickedly, reading her mind, but made no comment. Still he wouldn't let her talk. He had something big to tell her, he indicated.

"I know, Domingo said...."

He leaned across the table and took both her hands in his, turning them up as though he were going to read her palms again. But then after a moment he set them down gently and asked, "You remember the woman who came to the Starlight Room with me? Mrs. Berenstein?"

She was taken completely by surprise and could only nod. What on earth was he going to tell her? She steeled herself for any confessions he might make.

"She's a scout for Sam Gregory."

He sat back, gaze fixed on her face, with the air of someone who had just made an astounding statement and was waiting for a reaction.

She stared at him blankly for a minute, then sat up straight, as though a jolt of electricity had gone through her. "The variety and talk show on television? I've watched it sometimes. Last week—" She broke off, eyes widening. "*Michael!* Sam Gregory wants Domingo on the show? That's what all this is about? That's great! No wonder Domingo was—"

"Not just Domingo," he interrupted.

"The whole group?"

"Including you. Especially you. Mrs. Berenstein

caught the session on Saturday and complained it wasn't as good without you. She was very impressed by your singing."

"She didn't look impressed." Blythe couldn't take it in. She couldn't believe....

"So the woman's a little jaded. That doesn't mean she doesn't recognize talent when she hears it. When you and Eddie sang together...."

"'The Sam Gregory Show,'" Blythe repeated excitedly. "I watched it last week while I was home. Ray Parker, Jr. was on. It's a national show, tremendously popular."

"Exactly."

"But Michael, I was going to quit. I'd just about made up my mind that I couldn't go on. Craig and David—"

His dark eyebrows had drawn together. "You still haven't broken with Craig?"

"Of course I have. I told him I didn't feel the same about him."

He shook his head. "Oh, Daisy, Daisy, what am I going to do about you? You're keeping one foot back in the cage, aren't you? Why? Security?"

She suspected that his suggestion was uncomfortably close to the truth, but she couldn't admit as much to him. "Craig and I are still in business together," she pointed out, then exclaimed, "Can you imagine what this is going to do to my time? Domingo's going to want extra work. We're supposed to use original material?"

He nodded. "You have exactly one month to get ready."

"Domingo invited me to help with the songs. I've always wanted to write songs. Oh, gosh, there must be thousands of singers who'd give their right arms for an opportunity like this. There's no way I can turn it down. I *have* to say yes!"

He leaned forward, cupped her face with his hands and kissed her gently on the mouth. "That's what I hoped you'd say."

A young suntanned waiter arrived to take their order, and Blythe gazed blankly at the large harbor excursion boat loaded with sightseers that had just gone by the end of the pier. The sun struck diamond flashes of brilliance from the silver-gray water in the boat's wake. Beyond the boat, the Coronado Bay Bridge curved gracefully over to the island. "You did want to try the clam chowder?" she heard Michael ask, and she nodded blindly.

"The Sam Gregory Show." She was suddenly terrified. "Is Domingo sure I'm good enough?" she blurted out.

Michael laughed. "Daisy strikes again." He looked at her intently. "Domingo's sure. I'm sure. Mrs. Berenstein's sure." His hand covered hers warmly on the table. "You'll be great, Blythe." He looked abruptly rueful. "I may regret setting this up. Once the country hears Temptation, offers will be pouring in. I'm probably going to lose the best group I've ever had. Business has doubled at Chez Michel since I hired the group."

"You think Domingo will accept other offers?"

"Of course he will. He'd be crazy if he didn't."

His glance caught hers, then moved away, and she thought, *what if the offers include me, Michael? Will my singing be such a wonderful thing to you, then? Will you act like Craig? He used to praise my singing, still does, but he doesn't like the fact that I'm singing for Domingo, even though he won't admit it.* Of course,

Craig's attitude was colored by his jealousy of Michael, for which he certainly had ample grounds. Poor Craig.

No, it was foolish to compare the reactions of the two men. After all Michael's efforts on her behalf, he'd hardly try to stop her from going on to bigger and better opportunities. He'd be more likely to just let her go, his Pygmalion project completed—Daisy released from her cage, free and independent in the big wide world. She sighed. Why was it that whenever something wonderful happened it brought problems in its wake as surely as the sea gulls following the excursion boat out there?

"This is supposed to be a celebration, Blythe," Michael said, and she forced herself to smile at him.

"I'm celebrating," she replied. "I just haven't recovered from the shock enough to show it yet. It's too sudden, I guess, too unexpected." She gave him a more genuine smile. "I haven't even thanked you for arranging for Mrs. Berenstein to come."

"You can thank me later." He accompanied this statement with such a deliberately leering glance that she laughed aloud.

"I thought you didn't want gratitude."

"It has its place." He hesitated, then slanted a teasing glance at her. "You thought I was living up to my reputation, didn't you? When you saw me with Mrs. Berenstein? What was it you called me? A philanderer?"

"I thought you might be involved with her, yes," she confessed. "You did admit to a preference for older women. I wondered though why you weren't paying more attention to her."

"How could I?" he asked, and his eyes were as eloquent as always. She wished suddenly that he wouldn't look at her like that, so lovingly. It made her heart leap with hope, and she wasn't going to be stupid enough to start hoping. Michael Channing cared about her; she could tell that. He wanted her to be happy. If he didn't, he'd hardly have arranged this wonderful chance for her. But that didn't mean he was madly in love with her, or even mildly in love with her.

She forced a laugh, then accepted the glass of champagne he offered her. She hadn't even noticed that the waiter had brought it. "In the middle of the day?" she queried.

"I thought we'd play hooky," he said. "There's Seaport Village right there. We could walk around, maybe ride the carousel...."

"Aren't we a little old for that?"

"Speak for yourself."

"I guess you aren't 007, after all," she said lightly. "You're really Peter Pan, the little boy who never grew up."

Unexpectedly a shadow darkened his face. Something in him withdrew from her as it had done once before. There was suddenly no life or expression in his face. "I'm grown up, Blythe," he said curtly.

"Well, I know that. I just meant... well, you don't always act grown up."

He looked at her. "Don't confuse playfulness with childishness," he said, and his voice was still tight and unnatural.

Taken aback, she stared at him. "Michael, I didn't mean to insult you. I was teasing."

For a second longer the expressionless mask stayed on his face. Then he shook his head as though to clear it and lifted his champagne glass to touch hers. "We have to start our celebration," he said firmly, warmth returning to his dark eyes. "What about it? Will you ride the carousel with me? It's around a hundred years old, you know. Well, of course you know. I keep forgetting you're a tour guide."

Was it impossible for any of her men to remember that there were several facets to her life? Did she have to be slotted in Michael's mind as a singer, in Craig's as a tour guide? "I should go home and do some bookkeeping," she said slowly. "I'm sure Julie's done a good job, but . . . ."

"You think you'd be able to keep your mind on your work?" Michael asked.

"Probably not." She laughed suddenly. It was her day off, after all. Craig and David were working on one of the buses, but she couldn't do much to help there. And anyway, it was probably good for her to be out in the fresh air after a week of incarceration. *Rationalizing*, she thought weakly, at the same time as she said, "Okay, the carousel it is," to Michael.

His answering grin was merry, and she wondered again about that moment of annoyance. No, "annoyance" wasn't the right word. He'd seemed... distant, lost.

She realized abruptly that she hadn't been able to learn for sure if his interest in her *was* partly due to her voice. As soon as he'd told her about Sam Gregory, she'd known she couldn't let the group down, couldn't let herself down. She hadn't been able to stick to her decision to quit. So she was no nearer knowing how Michael really felt about her, or closer to understanding his motivations. She sighed inwardly. He'd never pretended to have any motivations other than pleasure. It gave him pleasure to kiss her and make love to her. It gave him pleasure to make her fantasies about singing come true. He wanted her to believe in fairy tales. Quite obviously there was nothing deeper involved as far as he was concerned.

"Blythe," he said in a warning voice, and she obediently lifted her glass and sipped the cool liquid. The champagne bubbles tickled her mouth, and at the same moment a sudden little breeze disturbed the line of pennants flying above the restaurant, making them snap loudly. Camelot, she thought helplessly. Always Camelot. Yet it was virtually impossible to feel depressed on such a cloudless day, when she was here with the man she loved, drinking champagne and finally absorbing the knowledge that she was, she really was, going to sing on national television.

"To Temptation," she said impulsively, raising her glass, not caring that Michael would make out of her toast yet another double entendre.

Which he did. His slow smile glinted in his eyes, and he leaned toward her, kissing her lightly on the mouth before taking a sip of his champagne. "To temptation," he echoed gravely, and she felt a now-familiar thrill of sensation go through her at the seductive promise in his voice.

THEY DID RIDE THE CAROUSEL. Blythe had often watched while tourists' children rode the vintage horses, but she certainly hadn't wanted to try it herself, not in recent years, anyway. It was probably sixteen years since she'd ridden any kind of carnival ride. She had forgotten how much fun it was to ride up and down and around while the brassy music played. Across the space between their painted horses, Michael held her hand. Her hair blew free, and she felt herself smiling like a child, carefree and happy in the sunshine of a golden afternoon.

Michael's answering smile was just as carefree. He was really a wonderful companion. Did it matter that sooner or later their delightful time together would have to come to an end? Eventually she would have to face heartbreak, but in the meantime, was it really so wrong just to enjoy being with this man?

On their second ride, a couple of dark-haired little girls in minuscule T-shirts and blue jeans started waving to them every time they went by. Blythe and Michael both waved back, and when the carousel stopped, Michael signaled her to stay put, got down and, after speaking to the children's obviously pregnant mother, lifted both girls up on the platform, then settled one in front of Blythe and one with him. Blythe held tightly to the little warm body, delighting in the child's laughter. For a few moments Blythe fantasized that she and Michael were married and the children were theirs and they were all out together on a family outing. Even if she hadn't become emotionally involved, she'd have thought it was too bad that Michael Channing wasn't the marrying kind. He seemed to enjoy children and to have a rapport with them. She remembered him talking to the little boy and his sister in Tijuana, and now he was looking down at the ecstatic little girl in his arms, listening to her chatter with the kind of grave attention children loved.

After the ride was over, the children ran from the carousel to their smiling mother, and Michael and Blythe spent an hour exploring the many little shops of the village. Blythe had always enjoyed the feeling of Old Monterey, Victorian San Francisco and traditional Mexico that had been combined to create tourist magic in Seaport Village. With Michael she saw it as a child might, as a place to have fun. He made her try on a ridiculous yellow felt hat with a green feather in it, then bought it for her, ignoring her protests, and made her wear it. He bought her a windup bath toy, an even more ridiculous green frog that did the backstroke when wound with a key. They shared an ice-cream cone and she bought him a T-shirt with Macho Man printed on the back. At last he steered her toward a glass boutique that he said held a surprise for her. She tilted her hat over one eye. "You really think I need any more surprises today?"

He laughed. "This one is special." He kissed her nose lightly. "I promise you don't have to wear it."

The store was small, but brilliantly lighted to display its wares. On one side were crystal glasses and pitchers and vases; on the other two walls, a collection of animals and birds of all kinds and sizes. A plump, brown-haired, middle-aged woman with a very warm smile was the only occupant. She was carefully tidying up the shelves. A tour bus had just left, she told Michael. The people had bought very little but handled everything. "I guess I'll never get over worrying that people are going to smash my entire inventory," she said cheerfully. "No one ever has, but I die a thousand deaths if there are more than two people in the store." Her smile widened and she looked at Michael with sudden recognition. "You're the gentleman who came in a few days ago? You own the restaurant on the pier?"

Michael nodded.

"He's all finished," the woman went on. "I've got

him stashed in the back room for safety. I'll bring him out right away."

Blythe looked at Michael questioningly as the woman bustled out of sight through a door in the back of the store. He shook his head, smiling mysteriously, and she turned her attention to the shelves of animals. They were beautifully crafted...rabbits, frogs, seals, cats, a sea gull caught in midflight. Blythe went from one to another, exclaiming over their beauty.

The woman returned in time to hear her. "Now, dear, I'm not averse to flattery, but let's not get carried away. What do you think?" she asked Michael. "Is he the way you wanted him?" She laughed. "I'm very partial to him myself. He's a fine specimen, don't you think?"

Michael took the glass object she'd brought out of the back room and held it up to the light for Blythe to see. At first she thought it was a horse. He stood about eight inches high, rearing up on his hind legs, his front legs pawing the air. He might have been alive, there was so much vigor in the arrogant tilt of his head, the bold eyes and the curling, jagged mane. His tail might just have flicked defiance at some other warring male. It was remarkable how lifelike he was. Though he was made completely of clear glass, there was a sense of muscle below the surface, an impression of bone and sinew. Blythe could almost imagine warm breath coming from the flared nostrils.

She held out her hands and Michael set the animal carefully in her grasp, and she saw that it was not a horse, after all. From the middle of his forehead a long twisted horn protruded. "A unicorn," she exclaimed, then laughed, looking at Michael. "I might have known."

"A wondrous beast," Michael intoned. "In medieval times he was considered to possess great strength and fierceness. I wouldn't be at all surprised to learn that he once lived in Camelot. Why else would he show up on the royal arms?"

"It's too bad he never really existed," Blythe murmured.

"Of course he existed," Michael said. "He still exists. So does Camelot."

"In imagination."

"Which is as valid a place as any to live."

"But not very practical," she objected.

He sighed. "No, not practical. He's for you," he added. "To celebrate your new career."

"'New career'?"

"As a television star."

"I'm hardly a star," she protested. She glanced down at the unicorn. "Is he really mine? He's beautiful. Thank you, Michael."

He didn't answer, and she looked at him over the unicorn's head. He had left his suit jacket and tie at the restaurant and still had his shirt open at the collar, the sleeves rolled up. He was looking at her with the intent, deliberately seductive gaze that always sent her blood pressure rocketing. "Some people believe if you give a woman a unicorn she'll be enchanted with you forever," he said softly.

The store owner giggled, then discreetly walked away to the other side of the store and started rearranging some decanters. "I've never heard that," Blythe said.

"Probably because I just made it up."

"You want me to be enchanted with you *forever*?" she asked with a lift of one eyebrow.

He was still holding her gaze and he continued to do so for a moment longer. Then his own eyebrows slanted upward and his smile broke through. "Well, through next week, anyway."

Quicksilver, she thought as she had once before. "I warn you, Michael Channing," she managed to say lightly. "If you continue to ply me with gifts, I may stay enchanted with you for a year or more."

"I'll try to bear up," he said promptly.

She looked quickly at his face. He was still smiling. She sighed. What had she been trying to do... pin him down to a commitment? Didn't she know yet how impossible that was?

THEY SAT ON A BENCH by the pond in the central plaza, enjoying the sound of water rippling over smooth flat rocks, the play of sunlight and shadow, the excited twittering of birds in a nearby tree; the glass unicorn sat safely wrapped and boxed and stowed on the bench between them. The village was emptying out now, the tourists returning to their hotels for dinner, children going home for the night. Both Michael and Blythe seemed to feel the same reluctance to leave the sunny area. Perhaps because after today Blythe's time would be taken up once more with tour duties and rehearsals and performances. She'd be lucky to find time to breathe, let alone play hooky with Michael again.

As they sat there, the two little dark-haired girls went by with their mother. They both waved and the mother called, "Thank you again," and smiled at Michael.

Michael's answering smile lingered as he watched the little girls walking along the red cobbled path, stopping now and then to talk to the waddling pigeons. "You like children, don't you?" Blythe said warmly.

He didn't reply for a moment, and she glanced at him and saw that his smile had disappeared abruptly. "Don't you, Michael?" she persisted, and he moved a little on the bench and said, "Yes," with no inflection in his voice at all.

Why such a terse answer, she wondered. Had he thought she was hinting at a possible future for them?

He was looking at her now with a speculative expression. "You're not pregnant, are you?" he asked.

She felt chilled all the way through. "Of course not. I was just making an observation." She hesitated. "You don't need to worry. I'm on the pill. My doctor started me on it several years ago because I had irregular periods."

Her voice had reflected her distress that he should misinterpret her remark, and he was obviously immediately conscious that he'd upset her. "I'm sorry, Blythe," he said, reaching across the package to take her hand. "I wasn't thinking, I guess. I didn't mean to...." He paused, then frowned at her. "What would you do? If you did get pregnant?"

Astonished, she stared at him. He was looking at her intently, as though her answer were very important to him. Why? "I'd have the baby and raise it of course," she said firmly. "I love children," she added. "I intend having at least two someday. But you don't have to worry," she repeated. "I am protected and—"

"I'm sorry, Blythe." The bleak look had left his face and his hand was gripping hers tightly. As she continued to stare at him, he lifted the package from between them and set it down on his other side, moving over to sit closer to her. "I think I should explain to you," he began, then hesitated again. "I want you to understand something about me. So I have to tell you...."

"Is this to do with your marriage?" she asked gently.

He nodded, gazed for a moment at a nearby bush that was bright with clusters of red berries, then at a bed of tall cacti. "I've always wanted children," he said slowly.

"Why didn't you have some then?"

He swallowed. At first she thought he wasn't going to answer. Then he said very rapidly, as though he wanted to get the words out before changing his mind, "My wife *was* pregnant. About two and a half years ago. Things hadn't been going too well between us for some time, but we were trying to work through the bad patch. Then Ellie told me she was three-months' pregnant. I was so ecstatic I didn't notice she was less than enthusiastic. Or if I did, I put her lack of excitement down to discomfort. She was having some morning sickness. I should have been more alert, I guess, but I was too busy buying up baby clothes and furniture and painting—" his voice faltered and he took a deep breath "—painting the nursery."

He paused again. "One day I came home from work and found Ellie lying on the sofa watching television. That wasn't unusual. She spent a lot of time doing that. But I noticed she looked...wan. At first she didn't want to tell me what was wrong, but then she confessed she'd had an abortion."

"You mean she miscarried? She had a spontaneous abortion?"

"No. She'd gone somewhere. Our own doctor wouldn't do it for her because the...fetus was four-months' old."

"Dear God." She stared at him. "Was there something wrong with the baby? Some reason?"

He shook his head, not looking at her. "According to Ellie's doctor, it was a healthy fetus." He grimaced, his face tight with pain. "Excuse me, I have to refer to...it as a fetus. If I think of it as a child...my child...." His voice failed, and her heart went out to him.

"That's why you left her," she said.

He nodded. "I couldn't look at her afterward. I felt that she'd murdered my baby. She did murder my baby."

"Why did she? How could she?"

"She said she didn't want the responsibility of being a mother." He laughed shortly. "Ellie and I were very young when we married. We decided to wait to have a child until we were able to...." He sighed. "She kept putting it off. I was beginning to worry that we might have left it too late. But I loved her. She was so winsome. Sweet and happy always. Never lost her temper. And I thought she loved me. She said she did. Until then. Then she confessed she didn't want to be married anymore. She wanted to be free. Marriage wasn't any fun. She'd been horrified to discover she was pregnant."

His eyes held the distant, lost look again. He didn't speak for a while, and when he did his voice was strained. "I didn't realize until too late that our playfulness together masked the fact that she didn't want any responsibilities at all. She was the female equivalent of Peter Pan, I guess."

She drew in her breath. "I'm sorry, Michael. I would never have said—"

"You couldn't know." He attempted a smile that didn't make it to his eyes. "I'm sorry. I just suddenly wanted to tell you so you'd understand why I can't—" He broke off. "I've never told anyone before." He took a deep breath. "I've always believed in a woman's right to decide what should happen to her own body. And I guess I've gone along with the legalizing of abortion. It was far better, I thought, for a woman to have professional help if an abortion was what she wanted. I may even have said as much to Ellie. But I couldn't ever feel that way about my own child. When I found out, I went crazy for a while, I guess. I thought I'd never trust a woman again. I'm still not sure I'll ever be able to."

She tried to imagine it, to feel his pain. To come home one day and be told that your unborn child—a baby you wanted, a baby you already loved—had been...done away with as though it had no value.

No wonder he'd dated older women who were more...responsible.

"Oh, Michael," she said helplessly. "How can you still believe in fairy tales?"

"I have to," he said simply, and she saw that his eyes were dark with tears. She reached to hold him close to her. It was ironic in a way, she thought, sitting there. She had thought she'd never understand him. And now she did. But any hope of a permanent bond between them was farther away than ever. Having gone through such an experience, how *could* he be expected to trust any woman again? How could he ever trust love again? He would never commit himself emotionally. He would love only as long as the love was light and he could escape into a fantasy world. Camelot, a place where knights saved fair damsels in distress and chivalry was rewarded with favors. He'd even told her, early in their relationship, that he'd always covered up deep feelings by clowning around. Sooner or later she would reveal to him with some unguarded statement or gesture that she loved him deeply, and then she would lose him, and the loss would break her heart.

LATER THAT EVENING, Blythe tried to offer him comfort with her body, because she had no words to help him with. They had driven to his house in La Jolla. Together they'd prepared dinner and eaten it in front of the fireplace. A strong sea breeze had come up, chilling the air, and Michael lit a fire in the fireplace. They were able to talk as easily as always, though by mutual consent they avoided the subject he'd brought up in Seaport Village. They talked instead about Mrs. Berenstein and "The Sam Gregory Show" and Domingo and his talent and Blythe's own fears about the performance. On the surface, Michael was his usual entertaining self, but something had changed between them. Having revealed his pain to her, he couldn't just hide it again under a facade of lightheartedness, no matter how hard he tried.

After they'd eaten, he set the small table aside and pulled Blythe down to sit with him on the bearskin rug. It wasn't really a bearskin, he explained, with a self-deprecating smile. It was a good synthetic, bought because he loved the luxurious silkiness of fur but couldn't bring himself to buy a skin that had once covered a live animal. She felt her heart swell at this further proof of his sensitivity.

Inevitably, after holding each other close in the firelight for a while, they began to make love. There was a kind of sweet sadness to their lovemaking that had not been present between them before. They undressed each other slowly, playfully, but it was more like a rite than a game. As they talked and kissed, a feeling of certainty wrapped itself around her, a feeling that he was preparing to put her out of his life. She felt terribly afraid, anticipating the empty loneliness that would be hers if her suspicions proved to be true.

The firelight gleamed on Michael's cheekbones and in the blue-black depths of his hair. It highlighted the creamy ivory of Blythe's body, casting shadows that made their act of love seem more mysterious, more tender than ever before. Michael knelt above her, his face solemn, and took her face between his hands, cupping it carefully as though it were made of precious porcelain and might break if he pressed too hard. Slowly he moved his fingertips over her face, as though he were trying to memorize her features. She submitted to his gentle search in silence, unable to put her fear into words.

After a while, his fingers moved across her throat and down to her body, delicately sliding over her breasts to her waist, then tracing the faint line that ran from her navel on downward, following his fingers more vigorously with his lips and tongue. She held him tightly at the neck, feeling every hard insistent kiss in the depths of her being, welcoming the continual exploration of his tongue and hands that drove thought away and made her tense with excitement.

As pressure mounted inside her, his mouth slid across her breasts; his tongue lightly traced the pale-blue veins from the outer circumferences to the erect nipples. "Lovely Blythe," he kept murmuring.

She tried hard to change the words in her mind to "I love you," but her efforts were unrewarded. Inevitably, as she had expected and feared, she heard her own voice say the words as he entered the warm moistness between her thighs. "I love you, Michael. I love you."

His body tensed for a second. Then his head lifted and he looked at her. The firelight reflected in his narrowed eyes and she saw that he was smiling, but his mouth was wry. And then he lifted her to him and moved inside her. Her pulses were pounding and her body was lifting and falling, controlled by his hard hands and the rhythms of his body. It didn't seem to matter anymore if he loved her or not. He was *making* love to her and that, for now, was enough.

Against her back the silky black rug felt like sun-warmed grass caressing her flesh, as she arched and relaxed her body in time with Michael's. Above her, beyond Michael's smooth tanned shoulder, the shadows on the cathedral ceiling blurred and flickered like leaf shadows cast by spring sunshine. She could hear his voice in her memory saying, "In a faraway place and time. England, perhaps. Camelot. In the moonlight."

Her blood thrummed through her veins and she locked herself against him in a grip that could surely never be broken. She wanted to become a part of him, to stay close always to the clean scent of his skin, her hands pressed to the straining muscles of his back, his mouth on hers as it was now, his breath mingling with hers, two people becoming one.

Still the pressure built inside her, tensing her body until it was rigid under his. His own body had tightened. There was an instant of stillness, and then the pressure exploded in both of them at the same moment in a great shudder that threatened to tear them apart but instead brought them closer together, so that they seemed finally to be one at last, joined not only where their bodies and hands and mouths touched, but sharing the same complex system of arteries and veins and nerves.

"I love you, Blythe," Michael said against her shoulder.

She had longed to hear those words, but now that he'd said them, she felt a familiar aching emptiness return. The sadness had not disappeared from his voice. The words had come out of him as though they'd been dragged from his soul against his will. They sounded like goodbye.

8

THREE WEEKS PASSED in a blur. Every day Blythe told herself she would break the news about "The Sam Gregory Show" to Craig and David. Every day she found some reason for delay.

Her reasons were valid enough. She had never worked so hard in her life. There wasn't a spare or free minute in her day. Besides her regular duties for Wanderlust and her weekend performances in the Starlight Room, she had to fit in longer rehearsals with Temptation and brainstorming sessions where the group worked together on new material, arguing, revising, criticizing. At first Blythe made suggestions tentatively, then with more conviction. Soon she was an accepted member of the songwriting team. She had never thought of trying to create songs with someone else before. It was the most stimulating experience she had ever had. Stacey might suggest a string of notes, some rhythmic phrases. Domingo would pick them up on the guitar, expand them. Blythe would softly sing the words, trying them out, changing them, adding to them. Eddie would tape everything, play it back, offer some suggestions of his own. Sometimes Blythe had the initial idea—thrilling when the rest of the group went winging off with it, changing and rejecting chords and rhyme schemes but staying with her conception. Together during that period they wrote six songs, then selected two for "The Sam Gregory Show," honing them until they were all satisfied they were the best they could do.

Following these late-afternoon sessions, usually held at Domingo's because his small house had a basement and they wouldn't disturb the neighbors, Blythe would drive home to her apartment at the highest speed the law allowed. If it was a weekend, she'd hurriedly shower and change and be off to the Starlight Room. On weekdays when the sessions lasted until seven or eight in the evening, she'd race off to meet Michael. Sometimes they went out to dinner and on to the symphony or the opera; sometimes they went jogging on the beach, then returned to Michael's beautiful house, gleaming with perspiration, not stopping to take a shower before making love because their desperate need of each other was too urgent.

Afterward they lay together, his hands stroking her, while she kissed his warm, moist shoulder, her hand pressed to the soft hair that covered his still-pounding heart. He told her repeatedly that he loved her. She told him the same. That time she had been sick she'd thought that when—if—he said the words, she would be the happiest woman in the world. And it was true that his declaration contented some small dreaming part of her. But she wanted more. She wanted promises of forever, promises he was not prepared to make.

She was rarely at home. Sometimes she hauled herself up the steps to the apartment at two in the morning and dropped into bed the moment she pulled off her clothes. She slept without dreaming, woke the instant the alarm sounded, pushed herself into beginning another day. She began to feel like the character in Stephen Leacock's story who "flung himself upon his horse and rode madly off in all directions."

Michael noticed her exhaustion where nobody else did. "Maybe we shouldn't see each other for a while so you can rest," he suggested.

He was holding her in his arms in his wonderfully comfortable water bed. A moment before she had felt wildly, radiantly overheated, but abruptly she was chilled. She held on to him tightly, kissing him until he complained with a smile that he was totally out of breath. She couldn't let him go, not yet.

In the days that followed, she redoubled her efforts to seem alert and energetic when she was with him. Even though she suspected the carousel ride would soon be over, the music would stop, the painted horses would still their prancing and the lights would go out one by one, she couldn't bear the thought of being apart from him on those rare occasions when her time didn't belong to someone else. During the few hours she slept each night, she dreamed that she was running, always running.

It was inevitable that eventually her body would rebel.

She was driving back from Tijuana on a Thursday. A light rain was falling and the windshield wipers were thrumming hypnotically. Blythe felt hot and mildly nauseated. She hadn't eaten very much in the previous week. Her stomach had apparently shrunk, or else nervous tension had damaged its ability to handle food. Suddenly a bright-red Porsche darted in front of the minibus. Traffic ahead was heavy and slowing. She saw at once that she didn't have room to brake, but it was another second or two before her brain interpreted the problem, and then it overreacted and she swung the wheel too hard, and the bus skidded on the rain-slick road and came to a halt facing in the wrong direction.

No one was hurt. Her passengers, somnolent themselves, were mildly shaken up, but put all the blame on the driver of the Porsche, who had already hightailed it out of sight. Blythe was able to drive safely and alertly the rest of the way home, but her hands wouldn't stop shaking. She knew the time had come to face Craig and her brother.

She waited until the next morning, at 8:30, when they were all gathered in the office, then told them calmly that she couldn't go on as she had and why.

"Television!" David exclaimed. "You're going on television?" He made it sound like an accusation.

There was a brief silence, then Craig, who had been standing with his back to the wall, let out a long breath and said, "Rehearsals. I thought all this time you were with Michael Channing." He was smiling.

"I was with Michael as much as possible," Blythe admitted, and his smile faded into a frown.

She glanced at David. He was looking at her sternly. "You've been trying to do far too much," he said. "I've wanted to tell you to slow down, but you were always on the run and I didn't have a chance."

"I thought I could do it all, Dave," she said softly. "I guess I thought I was Superwoman."

"So instead of giving up your new hobby, you want to give up the business," Craig said truculently.

Her new *hobby*! Blythe sat down in the customer chair beside the desk and looked up at him wearily. "I don't want to give up anything," she told him. "I just want a leave of absence until things quiet down."

"What if they don't quiet down?" His face was flushed with anger, his gray eyes stormy. "You've made promises before that you didn't keep. You weren't supposed to sing longer than two weeks."

Blythe sighed. Apparently he really believed she had made that promise. What was the use of arguing? "If things don't quiet down, then I'll have to think again."

He stood up very straight and tall, arms crossed on his muscular chest, looking like an executioner or a bouncer hired to throw obstreperous patrons out of a bar. "I've been very patient with you, Blythe," he said slowly. "I told you I'd wait, and I have been waiting. But I don't think I can wait much longer if you insist on seeing Michael Channing. You never have time for me anymore."

Blythe drew in a deep breath, then let it out. "I'm sorry, Craig, I should have told you right at the start, but I didn't want to hurt you." She paused, then plunged on. "I'm in love with Michael."

Across the desk she heard the swift intake of David's breath, but she didn't look at him. First she had to straighten things out with Craig. Then she could talk to her brother.

"You don't know what love is," Craig said flatly. "I love you and you don't even care."

"Of course I care." She glanced up at him, saw that he'd relaxed his stance and was gazing down at the floor, his face sorrowful and aggrieved. She recognized the expression. *Look how you've hurt me. If you'd only do what I know is right for you, all your problems would disappear.*

"You don't love *me*, Craig," she said quietly. "You tried very hard to turn me into someone you could love, but it didn't take."

She remembered suddenly how she'd defined true love to herself—two people working together toward a common goal, putting the other person first, understanding each other. She and Craig hadn't ever really shared a *common* goal—the goal had been Craig's, and he had tailored her to fit it. "You didn't ever *tell* me you loved me," she pointed out gently.

He was silent for a moment. Then his head came up and he shrugged. "What about the business?" he inquired sharply.

So much for love, she thought, then softened. She'd hurt him; he was just lashing out. "Maybe we could ask Julie. She seemed to enjoy working here when I was sick."

"We've already asked Julie to join us," David said quietly. "It's time to take on another person. We're getting enough demand to make it practical to buy another bus now. Julie's bored because Russ is away a lot, and as he won't accept help from her parents, they can use the money."

"You didn't tell me about the other bus—" Blythe began, but then she saw the look of condemnation in Craig's eyes and broke off. She could see what he was thinking. How could they have told her? She hadn't been around outside business hours long enough to be told anything.

"We'll still need to take on another person if you want some time off," David said evenly. "Craig and I have decided it makes sense to have someone in the office full time now, rather than switching around."

"You've decided an awful lot," Blythe started to say, then stopped again. Craig was probably right. She'd given up the right to complain about not being consulted. Was it worth it, she wondered, suddenly remembering the camaraderie that had once existed among them, the way it used to be when the three of them worked smoothly together, no one making a decision until they'd all had a chance to put their heads together. Her mind flickered images of them sharing cooking chores in the kitchen, sharing dishwashing, arguing for hours over tour routes and schedules.

"I'm sorry," she said weakly, though she wasn't sure what exactly she was apologizing for. Michael? Singing? Her television appearance?

"I have to go make the La Jolla run," Craig said abruptly, and started for the door.

"You've got fifteen minutes," Blythe pointed out. "We haven't reached any conclusions yet."

"Yes, we have." He turned at the door and looked at her bleakly. "You prefer singing to the business we built together. You prefer Michael Channing to me. What's left to discuss?"

He swung around before she could answer. A moment later the door slammed behind him.

Blythe stared at the closed door. "Is it so very terrible to want to sing?" she asked the empty air. She felt perilously close to tears.

David didn't speak, and she was afraid to turn around to face him, afraid she'd see the same condemnation in his eyes that she'd seen in Craig's. "I love singing, Dave," she said softly. "Can you possibly try to understand that? I've just recently realized that underneath I've always thought of myself as a singer, even when I wasn't doing much about it. That's who I am, what I am. A singer."

All of a sudden she felt a prickling in her eyes, a lump rising in her throat.

"Are you *crying*?" David asked abruptly.

The harsh sound of his voice was her undoing.

Her whole body started to shake and the threatened tears spilled down her face.

David was suddenly on her side of the desk, kneeling in front of her, pressing a tissue into her hand. "I can't believe this," he exclaimed. There was anger in his voice.

Hands to her face, she hunched her shoulders, trying to stop the tremors that were shaking her body. "I don't blame you for being angry," she mumbled. "I've let you down. I'm so sorry, Dave."

He made a small sound of . . . what? Disgust? Then he forcibly pried her fingers from her face, lifted her chin and made her look at him. His face was bleak, the skin stretched tight over his cheekbones. "'Sorry'?" he exclaimed. "My God, why should you be 'sorry'?"

Bewildered, she stared at him. "You're not angry? You *look* angry."

"I *am* angry. With myself, not you." He plucked another tissue from the box he'd brought with him, touched it to her eyes with infinite gentleness. "I can't believe Craig and I have been such selfish bastards. Lord, what we've put you through." He smiled at her lovingly, still mopping her face. "If you want to be a singer, sister mine, then that's what you're going to be. So stop crying before you drown both of us."

She stared at him incredulously. "You're *not* mad at me?" She managed what felt like a watery smile. "You make it sound so simple," she added.

"It is. Almost anyone with any intelligence can be a tour guide. Not that many can sing. You've got the talent and the opportunity. It would be criminal to waste either." He looked suddenly like the small boy she remembered from all the years of their shared childhood, mischievous and happy, without a care in the world. "Imagine, my sister a celebrity!" he exclaimed.

His face sobered abruptly. "I can't believe I've been so stupid," he said. "I've been going along with Craig, grumbling about the time you've taken away from us, not even realizing what a tremendous thing you were doing. You're really a success. Domingo thinks you're great. Sam Gregory wants you on his show. And all Craig and I can do is complain about the schedule and having to do more than our share of the cooking." There was disbelief in his voice.

"I tried to do my share," Blythe said miserably.

"I know you did. And I didn't even...." He was silent a moment, looking up at her with apology written all over his fair-skinned face. "I didn't even congratulate you," he said wonderingly. "You came in here and told us you were going on national television and I didn't even congratulate you."

"Nor did Craig," she said, biting her lip. "I knew he'd be upset, but I thought he might at least be pleased I'd got some recognition."

"And he's supposed to love you," David said. "I'm supposed to love you. I do love you." He stood up and pulled her up into a bear hug. "I'm so proud of you." He stepped back from her, holding on to her shoulders. "I am proud, Blythe. And I do congratulate you. And you aren't to worry about the business. You can take as much time off as you need, and if you want to come back, you can do so anytime."

"Craig might not agree."

"He'll agree." His voice was grim again. "The trouble with my good friend Craig is that he's too much like me. We've both protested how much we love you and want the best for you, but then we made it conditional. We'd only love you if you were the person we wanted you to be. When you grew wings and became yourself we withdrew all our support." He hesitated, looking at her affectionately. "Can you forgive me, Blythe? Can you forgive Craig? I'm sure he'll see the light as soon as I have a few words with him."

"I can't go back to loving Craig," she protested. "I mean, I do love him, the way I love you, like a friend, a brother."

"But you love Michael Channing more?"

"Yes."

He dropped her hand, walked around the desk and turned to face her, looking suddenly grim again.

Her newly resurrected optimism plummeted once more, and she sank back into her chair. But then he grinned sheepishly and said, "I've been holding out on you, Blythe."

Puzzled, she stared at him.

"I've been seeing a lot of Stephanie. Stephanie Goodwin." He emphasized the last name as though it held some special significance, but she didn't know what the significance could be.

She nodded uncertainly. "Julie's bridesmaid."

"Her father is Paul Goodwin."

"The banker?" She frowned for a moment, thinking. "He's quite a philanthropist, isn't he? Isn't he partly responsible for the restoration of the Gaslamp Quarter?"

"Along with several other citizens, yes. Including Michael Channing."

"Michael's working on it? I know he has a restaurant there, but he didn't tell me...."

"According to Stephanie he doesn't broadcast any of his good works. He just does them quietly and thoroughly. He's involved in numerous charities, especially those having to do with children." He sighed deeply. "I've had to revise my estimate of Michael Channing, Blythe. I liked him okay, but I thought he was a lightweight. I said as much to Stephanie when I was complaining about your seeing him." He blushed when she glanced sharply at him. "I know, I shouldn't have discussed you with her, but Craig kept grumbling, and I thought at that time he was right. As usual, I wasn't looking beyond my nose."

He glanced down at the desk, his smile sheepish again. "Stephanie lambasted me. Evidently her father thinks very highly of Channing. And he's not the only one. It's common knowledge that Michael's father wanted him to be an attorney. When Michael decided that wasn't the life for him, he refused to take money from his father because he'd disappointed him. He'd made up his mind he wanted to establish himself in the restaurant business and he wanted to do it by himself. He worked day and night. He washed dishes and tended bar. He was a cashier and a waiter and a chef. He did all those jobs, not just to earn a living but so he could learn every aspect of the business. Paul Goodwin encouraged him and even financed him, but he told Stephanie that Michael paid him back way before the loan was due. He's brilliant, Paul says. And very ambitious."

Blythe felt stunned. She had known almost everything David had just told her. Michael had told her most of it himself. But he'd made it sound so different, as though it had been the easiest thing in the world to buy his own restaurant and then go on to acquire five more. *Oh, Michael,* she thought. *You were covering up again, weren't you?*

How could she have been so stupid as to believe

such an undertaking could be easy? Of course he had worked hard. He still worked hard. She suddenly remembered him telling her how the salad at Chez Michel was prepared, remembered his concern for the *sous-chef* at Michael's On The Pier, his interest in how Casa de Miguel would look to a tourist. He let no detail escape him. Why hadn't she seen that, when she could see it so easily now?

"I'm sorry, Blythe," David said. "Stephanie set me straight about Michael a couple of weeks ago, but I didn't tell you because I kept hoping you and Craig would get back together again. I didn't want to make him appear even more attractive to you. Not very noble of me."

"You weren't the only one to misjudge him," she admitted. "I loved him, and even I thought—" She broke off, suddenly filled with love and admiration for Michael Channing. In spite of a busy schedule that she hadn't even given him credit for, he had made time to help make her dreams come true. He had seen the yearning in her even when she hadn't recognized it herself.

She became aware that David was talking again about Michael. "Stephanie also told me that Channing's wife tried to take him for everything she could get," he said. "She ended up with far more than she was entitled to under the law, but Channing didn't contest the settlement. Nor did he ever tell anyone why he left her. There must have been a reason, no matter what Craig says about him just walking out on her."

"There was a reason."

He looked at her questioningly, but she shook her head and he didn't press her, though she could see he was curious.

"Does he love you?" he asked.

She nodded, then gave him a wry smile. "For now, anyway."

With compassion in his eyes, he said, "Stephanie did say her father thinks it unlikely Michael will ever marry again."

"He's a smart man, Paul Goodwin," she said.

"Maybe it'll work out," he said softly.

She nodded again, but she couldn't share his confidence. The man she loved was clearer than ever in her mind now, but he was still quicksilver. He could still suddenly disappear from her life.

THE FOLLOWING WEEK was easier on Blythe. Julie started working full-time in the office. She would start driving as soon as Craig and David had their new bus and managed to hire another employee. Blythe had time now to rest, time to sleep in after a late rehearsal. But she saw no more of Michael than she had before. Busy herself, always running from one set of duties to another, she hadn't realized how busy *he* was. Now, with the wisdom imparted by David via Stephanie, she saw how tremendously involved his life was. He apparently checked on each of his restaurants every day. Why hadn't she at least suspected his devotion to business when Domingo commented that he was no absentee landlord? There were also evenings when he was otherwise engaged. Charity work, she surmised and quietly checked the meeting times of some local causes. Sure enough, they coincided with Michael's absences. When she saw Michael, she castigated herself for her lack of perception, but he dismissed all her apologies. "I'd much rather appear in your eyes as a great lover than a successful restaurateur," he told her lightly.

"You are a great lover," she said at once.

Those irrepressible eyebrows of his lifted over glinting eyes. "Would you care to give me an opportunity to prove it?" he asked, and she did.

Their time together became a little more relaxed, even though she still had a feeling of impending doom. At least she wasn't constantly thinking that she should be at home, spending some time with Craig and David, catching up on bookkeeping; she wasn't constantly feeling guilty, except about Craig. She still felt very guilty about Craig.

Sometimes she caught Michael looking at her with an expression of deep sadness on his face. But when she met his gaze, the mask would descend over his eyes again, shutting out the light. And then he would pull her impulsively into his arms and make love to her with an intensity that left her breathless, as though time were running out. He never spoke about the future.

THE DAY OF TEMPTATION'S television debut dawned sunny and cloudless. Domingo and Stacey, Eddie and Blythe drove early to Los Angeles in Domingo's van, which was crowded with equipment. They were all tense except for Domingo, who was in high spirits, singing at the top of his lungs, apparently not concerned that he'd wear his voice out before the show began.

Several hours after their arrival, Blythe sat in a small room adjacent to the television studio. She was alone, her hands clasped together so tightly the tips of her fingers were bloodless. The other three were off checking their equipment. She was terrified. Rehearsal had gone well, but she was sure that she herself was going to be a disaster. She remembered

Domingo's first evaluation of her voice..."a bit sterile some of the time." What if she sounded sterile today? She *felt* sterile.

She wished Michael were with her. She'd asked him to come, but he'd told her he didn't want to appear to be taking credit for the invitation from Sam Gregory.

"But you did make it possible," she argued.

He shook his head. "Temptation's talent made it possible."

A sound at the door made her look up. A young man was standing there, holding a box wrapped in bright paper. "Blythe Sherwood?" he asked.

She nodded, smiling, glad of the distraction, and took the package from him, hoping Craig hadn't sent her an apology gift, as he'd done once before. She didn't want to have to feel guilty about Craig today. She tore the wrappings open, pulled out a rag doll dressed in green felt with a red-hooded cape. Around the doll's neck was a slender silver whistle on a thin white silk cord. There was no card. It wasn't necessary. Only Michael Channing would send her Red Riding Hood and a whistle to protect her against any wolf who might be prowling L.A.

Putting the whistle to her lips, she blew lightly for good luck. There was no sound, and she examined it more closely. A dog whistle. Was that symbolic? A whistle that couldn't be heard by human ears?

Before she could argue herself out of the sudden depression that thought brought, the door opened again. For a heart-stopping moment she thought Michael might have answered the whistle even if he couldn't hear it. She could almost hear him telling her the sound was meant only for princely ears.

"You're on," the assistant producer told her, and

she reluctantly put down the doll, smoothed the plunging collar of her hot-pink jump suit and followed the young woman out. And then turned around hurriedly, pulled the whistle from the doll's neck and hung it around her own.

Michael was there, sitting in the audience, right in the front row, looking as lean and attractive as always in his dark suit, his black hair casually disarranged, his smile quizzical, loving, infinitely endearing. As she took her introductory bow, he put two fingers to his lips in imitation of a whistle, and she touched the cord around her neck, letting him know she understood he'd heard her call, after all.

She stepped to her mike next to Eddie. Domingo stepped to his. Wild rock streamed from his guitar. She and Eddie began to sing "Give It to Me," the song they'd all agreed was their most rousing. The audience went wild. They shouted and applauded. Some girls at the back of the studio started dancing. Blythe could feel excitement coming at them in waves from everyone in the room. Sam Gregory in his mock-up lounge at the side of the stage was beaming approval.

When they finished the applause was deafening. Eddie took his bows alongside her, whispered, "Go get 'em, Blythe," then retreated to his drums, leaving her alone. They had planned their next number carefully. A slow ballad—a contrast to the hard-rock opening number—to show their versatility. Blythe had hoped they might select the one song she'd been most responsible for, but Domingo had felt, regretfully, that it lacked enough universality for this important debut. The song they had chosen instead had been prompted by Blythe, but Stacey had done most of the work on it, showing a deep sensitivity that hadn't surprised her. It was called "Sweet Sadness." She sang it with a full heart and knew instinctively that she had never sung so well.

"This is only the beginning, you know," Michael said in the plane on the way back to San Diego. He'd already had her ticket in his pocket when he arrived. He didn't want her making the slow trip back through rush-hour traffic. Even the plane was crowded with commuters.

Blythe smiled at Michael. "The beginning of what?"

"Fame. Stardom. Whatever."

She shook her head, still smiling, still feeling high from the tremendous reception Temptation had received. She thought she'd handled herself fairly well in the interview portion of the show. Sam Gregory had reminded her a little bit of her father and she'd felt at ease with him, which was just as well... Domingo had suddenly turned shy as soon as he was expected to talk. "Maybe nothing will happen," she said.

"It will happen." There was conviction in his voice.

They sat in companionable silence for a few minutes. Then Michael said, "I want to ask you something, Blythe."

She looked at him questioningly, feeling suddenly as though the plane had hit an air pocket and left her stomach behind. He looked very solemn. And very dear. Impeccably suited as always, and wearing a white shirt and the Hermès tie she'd once told him was her favorite, his dark hair attractively tousled so that she knew he must have combed it with his fingers again, he looked very much like the gambler she'd once thought him. He had an air about him that said he was going to chance his whole bankroll on the next turn of the wheel. "I want you to consider moving in with me," he said.

"To your house?" she said stupidly.

His smile was strained. "I wasn't thinking of taking up residence in one of my restaurants."

Blythe swallowed and sat back in her seat, looking blankly at the top of the magazine that was poking out of the pocket on the back of the seat in front of her. Her primary reaction was amazement, and it was being closely followed by disappointment. "In Camelot?" she murmured.

"Exactly."

She found she didn't know what to say. She couldn't believe she wasn't wildly happy about the idea. If she'd suspected he was going to ask her to live with him, she'd have thought she would throw her arms around his neck and tell him that of course she'd come live with him. She wanted to live with him. And she didn't think she suffered from any moral inhibitions. No one would be hurt. David would understand.

Why was she hesitating?

Because she wanted marriage, she finally admitted to herself. No matter how many people scoffed that the "little piece of paper" wasn't necessary, in her mind marriage meant that two people were taking responsibility for their love. It meant they wouldn't go their separate ways if some small thing went wrong. They'd work it out together. It meant that they were committed to each other, committed to caring for each other in sickness as well as health, through financial misfortune, or earthquake, fire and flood.

If she moved in with Michael, she would be saying goodbye to her dream of children. She could never bear an illegitimate child. A child needed security, hungered for security. She knew that from her own experience.

"You want to think about it for a while?" Michael asked.

She nodded, and he sighed. "Well, I guess that's better than outright rejection."

She looked at him. "I've thought for a while that you were getting ready to reject me," she said.

"I was." How dark his eyes were when he wasn't smiling. Most of the time they were so full of light that she didn't even think about their color, but when he was solemn or hurting, they looked almost black, like a night sky without any stars.

"After I told you about Ellie," he said hesitantly, "I decided it wasn't fair to you to go on. You deserve someone without hang-ups, someone who doesn't expect you to live in...Camelot."

He paused, and to her relief his face warmed and the empty darkness receded from his eyes. The quizzical smile that she'd learned was usually self-mocking returned, and his straight eyebrows slanted into their inverted vee. "However," he said with a sigh, "though I want you to be happy, I found out that it's not so easy to be altruistic where you're concerned. I couldn't let you go."

"I don't want to be let go, Michael," she said softly.

Unsnapping his seat belt, he leaned across her without a glance at their fellow passengers and pulled her into his arms. A moment later their lips met, and Blythe felt the immediate rushing response that seemed to come from every part of her body to find expression in her mouth. He kissed her deeply and thoroughly, his mouth moving on hers, and once again she tried to banish reality and reason and lose herself in the world of her senses. She almost succeeded, but somewhere in a distant corner of her mind the thought persisted that she had a decision to make. Should she live with Michael, or lose him altogether? There was no doubt in her mind that if she turned down his invitation she would lose him. They could not go on as they were, trying to find a few minutes together whenever it was possible, constantly parting. Every relationship between a man and a woman had to change and grow, or sooner or later it would end.

9

BLYTHE SAT IN WANDERLUST'S OFFICE, her elbows on the desk, a silver pen Craig had given her the previous Christmas clasped between her fingers. The young woman David had sent over for her to interview had excused herself a minute ago to use the minuscule rest room, and Blythe was trying to decide why she felt so reluctant to make up her mind that the girl was worthy of employment.

The girl had excellent references. She'd worked at a travel agency since graduating from college a year ago. Her ex-employer had been sorry to lose her, but his office was in Seattle and she had wanted to come home to San Diego to be near her family. She was Stephanie Goodwin's sister, and David was becoming increasingly fond of Stephanie.

Added to all that was the fact that the girl... Blythe glanced at the application form in front of her—Bonnie Goodwin—was extremely attractive and bright, a pert brunette, slimmer than her sister, with a heart-shaped face, huge blue eyes and freckles. She'd look wonderful in the Wanderlust colors. David had been ready to hire her on the spot. So had Craig. But David had decided Blythe was entitled to an opinion, too.

They certainly needed to hire someone. April had turned into a very busy month, probably because winter seemed to be dragging on unusually long in many other parts of the country. And Blythe was even busier than before. True to Michael's prediction, Temptation had already received its first offers: a request to play for a benefit dance, an invitation to perform a concert in the university theater. Domingo's agent was negotiating other offers and he wanted the group to be ready. They'd already worked up some more new material and were revising and improving previous songs.

Blythe heard the sound of running water coming from the rest room. Any second Bonnie would reappear. Blythe had asked her enough questions. She had to make a decision. Now.

She'd had to make too many decisions lately, she thought, sighing. Michael was being very patient, waiting for her answer. She straightened in her seat and put the pen down on the desk. If she started thinking about Michael she'd never make up her mind about Bonnie.

"You think you'll be able to get along with David and Craig okay? And Julie?" she asked Bonnie when the girl returned and slipped into her seat with a bright smile.

She nodded vigorously, grinning. "I don't have any trouble getting along with anyone," she said. "I think it will be great to work with a bunch of people close to my own age. The last place the people were nice, but most of them were older, more settled, you know?"

Blythe nodded vaguely. "Well," she said finally, "Craig and David are very impressed by your credentials. And I am, too." She smiled at the younger woman. "Welcome to Wanderlust, Bonnie. You've got yourself a job."

Bonnie had a very attractive smile. It started

slowly in her eyes, moved gradually to her gamine mouth. "Thank you, Miss Sherwood," she said fervently.

Blythe made a face. "Call me 'Blythe,' please," she said. "I'm close to your age, too, remember. Craig's three years older, and David and I are twins."

"Sure. Sorry." She hesitated. "He's very handsome, isn't he?"

Oh, dear, Blythe thought, surely she wasn't falling for David. She must know that her sister—

"Did he play football in school?"

"Gosh, no. He's even more uncoordinated than I am. Neither of us was very good at sports, except for fencing, and we didn't exactly shine at that."

"He looks at though he played football," Bonnie said, smiling dreamily. "I like to read romance novels," she confessed. "Have you noticed how often the hero has gray eyes? I've never met a man with gray eyes before."

"You're talking about Craig?" Surprise made her voice almost strident.

Bonnie was frowning. "He's not...I mean, you and he aren't—Stephanie said that...." Her expression was one of charming confusion mixed with a tinge of disappointment. She really had the most expressive eyes.

Blythe grinned at her, suddenly feeling more lighthearted than she had in a long time. "So," she teased, "you like our Craig, do you?"

Bonnie nodded uncertainly. Her hands were nervously playing with the corded belt that sashed her white cotton dress. "I, er, don't know him very well, but he is awfully attractive. And nice, don't you think?"

"Very nice," Blythe said firmly. She really did feel incredibly lighthearted. Perhaps because she remembered that Craig had been certain Bonnie would do very well for Wanderlust.

She gave herself a mental shake. It wasn't exactly wise to matchmake even in her own mind, though if something did work out between Bonnie and Craig, she wouldn't have to go on feeling guilty anymore. It would be nice to have her worry about Craig off her mind. Though he'd been more himself since the TV show. He and David had both watched it and pronounced her performance fabulous. There had been a sheepish look around Craig's eyes when he congratulated her, and she suspected David had had the few words he'd promised. Craig had even kissed her lightly on the cheek and she'd realized then that for months before she met Michael she'd bracketed Craig in her mind with her brother. She suspected Craig felt the same way about her. Which was all to the good. Now they could go on being the family they'd always been.

She sighed. She certainly couldn't ever imagine feeling sisterly toward Michael. *Michael*. Whenever she was away from him, he kept coming alive in her mind, his wry face smiling at her, dark eyes glinting with devilish humor.

She became aware that Bonnie was gazing at her, still waiting for an answer to her stammered question. "I'm very fond of Craig," she said hastily. "I'm lucky," she added as the girl's face fell. "David's a wonderful brother, but it's nice to have a friend like Craig who can act in that capacity, too."

She'd never known freckles could glow before, she thought with amusement. Bonnie's heart-shaped face was positively beaming now.

EVERYTHING WAS FALLING INTO PLACE, she thought when she was back in the apartment, changing into blue jeans and a red scooped-neck T-shirt, ready for the rehearsal that would precede the evening performance at the Starlight Room. Bonnie would probably do a great job as a tour guide, and she and Craig just might get together. Yes, she was relieved that everything had been settled so nicely for Wanderlust, but all the same she did feel left out. She couldn't fool herself any longer that the change was temporary. With the hiring of Bonnie, Blythe had cut off most of the ties to her past. And Wanderlust would apparently thrive without her. She had thought she was indispensable, but she wasn't. Just as she might not be indispensable as far as Michael was concerned.

She had finished dressing; her jump suit was hanging in its garment bag, ready to go, and still she sat at her dressing table, gazing at herself in the mirror without really seeing her reflection. She was due at the Starlight Room in fifteen minutes. Michael would be there. Not for rehearsal, but for the evening session. He'd told her the previous day that he expected her to save him a dance. They hadn't danced in a long time, he'd complained with a glint in his eye. He had smiled as he said that, but underlying the smile she had seen something else. He wasn't going to press her to move in with him, but the question was always there.

She switched on the dressing-table lights and made an unnecessary adjustment to her hair, then caught sight of the glass unicorn shining in the light. He didn't really show to his best advantage here, she thought. He needed dark wood behind him, a light above. She'd tried him in several places in the apartment, but she hadn't yet found him a proper home. She picked him up and looked at him, remembering the day Michael had bought him for her, the day he'd told her about "The Sam Gregory Show," the day he'd told her about Ellie and what she had done.

It wasn't his fault he couldn't bring himself to trust in a long-term relationship again. When she thought about that little dead baby her heart ached for him. He loved her, she knew that for sure now. And the most wonderful thing was that he loved *her*, not some image of what she should be. More than anyone she'd ever known, he had encouraged her to realize her true potential. He had opened doors for her she could never have opened herself. And he'd given her so much. Joy. Wonder. The kind of child-like wonder he had himself. Never to be confused with childishness.

Something else. She'd lost her bitterness toward her parents. Learning to love Michael, learning how one person could become part of another, she'd understood how it had been with her mother and father. They had been too concerned with their own love affair with life to realize they weren't providing properly for their children. The fact that they hadn't been able to foresee an end to their charmed lives was surely not a major flaw in two otherwise lovable people.

Why did *she* have to be so damn practical, she wondered, sighing as she set the unicorn back on the dresser. Why did she have to constantly look ahead to see what the result of her actions would be?

Her eyes were watering, she realized. Much more of this introspection and she'd be bursting into tears again. She smiled down at the unicorn, who looked a little watery around the edges himself. "Michael loves me," she told him. "I love Michael. That's enough, isn't it? Doesn't he deserve some happiness? Why am I holding back?"

Because she was afraid, her mind responded instantly. She was emulating Daisy again, afraid to step out into an unexplored world. But she was right to be afraid. Like the unicorn, Michael was a fantasy figure, not a part of the world of reality. If she lived with him, she would wake up one morning to find that he had left her forever, that their love was like a dream that stayed in the memory but faded in the light of day. She would be alone. And if she *didn't* live with him, she would be alone. A no-win situation, as David would say.

She remembered wishing she could find a man as sensible as Craig who would stir her to the passion she'd found with Michael. Unfortunately no one was ever able to make a free choice about falling in love. She was no exception. It was no use wondering why that one particular mouth—Michael's mouth— affected her more than any other, why that one particular pair of hands—Michael's hands—gave her more pleasure. She wasn't going to fall in love with anyone else ever. Michael was it for her.

Suddenly she looked herself right in the eye in the dresser mirror. "If that's so," she said aloud, "if Michael's the one love of my life, why the hell shouldn't I enjoy whatever I can of him, while I can? Why the hell not?"

She ran a finger over the smooth back of the glass unicorn and stood up, suddenly feeling very defiant. "I'm going to tell him tonight," she said firmly. "And I know just *how* I'm going to tell him."

THE STARLIGHT ROOM WAS CROWDED. At Michael's urging, the manager of Chez Michel had moved in as many extra tables as fire regulations would permit. Since appearing on "The Sam Gregory Show," Temptation had become even more popular than before and reservations had been pouring in.

Michael came in halfway through the evening, as she was singing Domingo's song, "I Saw Him Walking." He sat down at a table that had been held for him, gave her the little two-fingered salute he reserved for her and sat back in his chair, his dark gaze watching her intently. As always, he seemed to exude sexuality and masculinity. The moment she saw him, tingling sensations raced through her body like fingers of fire and her heart quickened. She would always react to Michael this way, she suspected, always be assailed by this sudden weakness that spiraled upward and made the world tip on its axis. "How can I bear it if he walks away?" she sang, and her heart was in the words.

At the end of the number she signaled Domingo, as she'd arranged, and he began the intricate intro to the song she'd written, the song he'd decided wasn't universally appealing. But she hadn't written it for the universe.

She stepped up to the microphone. "Ladies and gentlemen," she said softly. Everyone in the audience turned to look at her. "I want to sing a different kind of song," she told them. "It's one I wrote myself—" she indicated Domingo and turned to incline her head toward Stacey and Eddie "—with a little help from my friends." There was a soft ripple of laughter, and she went on over it. "I'm dedicating it to someone who is very special to me. Someone who asked me a question. This is my answer."

She had his full attention. He was sitting very straight, looking directly at her, a frown lifting those irrepressible eyebrows of his. She saw that he hadn't yet drunk any of the wine he'd ordered, but was clutching the glass so hard he might possibly break the stem. "It's called 'The Glass Unicorn,'" she told him across the heads of the audience, and saw a slow smile start in his eyes.

She didn't take her gaze from him for a minute as she sang. Halfway through, she realized that the audience had caught on to the fact that *he* was the special person she'd mentioned. Glances were going from him to her and back again. No one was dancing, but most of the people were smiling.

Some part of her mind acknowledged all of this. Yet the thoughts were distant ones. Her whole concentration was involved in putting all her love into the words of the song. It was a soft melody with a lilt to it, what Domingo called a story song in the country tradition. It told of a woman who loved a man who believed in unicorns and princely frogs and Cinderella, a magical man who made dreams come true. It told of a land called never-never, where only two who loved could live together, and it ended, "I want to be there. I want to stay there. I want to live there...with you."

He stood up as she walked toward him. Every head in the place turned to watch. There was more shine in his eyes than usual. He took her outstretched hands in his and pulled her straight into his arms, kissing her without heed to the observers, who had already burst into pleased applause. Domingo immediately began a wild reggae number to turn attention back to the stage.

"Blythe," Michael murmured against her mouth. "Didn't I tell you that I hate crowds?" There was so much love in his voice that she caught her breath even as she laughed.

"I guess I did make a public spectacle of you," she admitted as they sat down.

He grinned at her. "I didn't mind at all. But I have to tell you I've changed my mind about you. I'm so—" He broke off and looked up as one of the waiters tapped him on the arm.

"Mr. Robinson and Mr. Elliott are here, sir," the waiter said.

"Damn," Michael exclaimed. "Some people have no sense of timing." He stood up, looked apologetically down at Blythe and said, "I'll have to ask you to excuse me. This is important. Don't go away now."

Stunned, Blythe watched his lean figure move away from her. What could be so important that he'd leave her at a moment like this? And what had he meant... "I've changed my mind." Had she made a terrible mistake? Had the public spectacle been of her?

Luckily, before she could speculate herself into a panic, Michael returned. There were two men with him. Mr. Robinson and Mr. Elliott, she presumed. One man was shorter than Michael by a head and completely bald. A nice-looking man for all that, if a bit overweight. He was smartly dressed in a blue pin-striped suit, starched shirt and tie. Gold glinted at his cuffs and in a chain that held his tie in place. The other man was younger, thinner and taller, shaggily blond and casual in a blue velour pullover and baggy pants. There was an aura of power about both of them.

Blythe expected Michael to bring the men over to his table, but instead he led them to the side table where Domingo and the other two members of the group had just sat down for their break. He introduced them all, the men sat down and all five immediately put their heads together and started talking. Domingo was waving his hands around excitedly. What on earth was going on?

"Where were we?" Michael asked as he sat down beside her.

"You said you'd changed your mind. Michael, what is—"

His fingers touched her lips to silence, and he called over a waiter and asked him to remove his glass of wine. "Bring some champagne, will you?" he called to the man as he turned away.

"'Champagne'?" Blythe echoed.

"We're celebrating again," he told her with a grin. And would say no more until the waiter returned and opened the bottle. He stopped him when he would have poured the champagne, picked up the bottle and glasses and held out his hand to Blythe. "Come with me," he said.

He had arranged to borrow the manager's office for a little while. The moment Blythe was inside, he closed and locked the door, grinning wickedly at her. Then he poured champagne into the glasses, handed her one and raised his own in a toast. She followed suit, still puzzled. "The older man is Arthur J. Robinson, known in the trade as A.J.," he explained. "The other is Buck Elliott."

"What trade?"

"The music trade. They're A & R directors."

"'A & R'.... Michael!" The glass in her hand tilted, threatened to spill. Hastily she set it down on the leather-topped desk. "That's the...an A & R director works for a record company. Artists and repertoire. He's the one who arranges for recordings to be made."

"Exactly. In this case, recordings by Temptation."

With a mischievous half smile, he set down his own glass, took her hands in his and added the name of a record company that Blythe knew had tremendous distribution.

Shocked almost speechless, Blythe could only stare at him for a minute. Then she reached up to kiss him softly on the cheek. "Michael, you're still making dreams come true."

He shook his head. "You can't have the kiss back, but I'm afraid I didn't wave the wand this time. A.J. saw you all on television." He grinned. "You are looking at your temporary manager. Subject to your approval, of course."

"I don't understand."

"It's very simple. As I told you once, I've been thinking it was high time I looked around me and saw my surroundings. Time to do a little traveling, let my managers get along without my interference for a while. Not all the time, but off and on, perhaps. Again subject to your approval."

Bewildered, she was still staring at him.

He grinned. "A.J. wants a whole album, Blythe. And he wants the group to tour when the album's released. I thought, if you have no objection, I'd come along when I could, help with the arrangements. It was Domingo's idea. It's up to you."

"But you said you'd changed your mind about me."

"Oh, yes, that. I've decided I don't want you to come and live with me in Camelot after all."

She drew back as though he'd struck her, and he laughed and pulled her into his arms. "Don't even think it, Blythe darling. Just hear me out, okay?"

She nodded, still stunned, and he set her away from him, looking into her face.

"When all of this came up...yesterday, Domingo started getting all excited and going on about the cities you'd all have to go to, and I found myself getting more and more depressed. How could you live with me if you were going to be on the road? Selfish, I know, but I'm being honest. That was my first thought. My second thought was that as I wouldn't dream of trying to persuade you not to go, I had to come up with a solution. You're climbing high, Blythe Sherwood, and nothing should be allowed to get in your way."

He paused and took a rather shaky breath, and she realized that although his hands were clasping her shoulders strongly, he was nervous about whatever he was going to say next. "Thinking about your going away from me, I realized that I hadn't offered you anything substantial to come back to. I've been hiding in Daisy's cage because I got hurt badly and was afraid I'd get hurt again. The only explanation I can find for my abominable conduct is that I haven't ever felt about anyone the way I feel about you. I've never felt such hunger for anyone. Or such love. I wasn't sure anything so amazing could be real or lasting."

He looked away from her, and his voice lowered. "Since I've known you I've felt that the world was filled with light, like a city at night, with hundreds, thousands of lights shining against the dark. When I realized you'd be going away and that you might not come back, I felt suddenly as though the lights had gone out everywhere and I was all alone in the dark."

"The painted horses stopped prancing," Blythe murmured.

The *look* in his eyes was something to behold.

"You, too?" he asked softly.

She nodded. "Me, too. That's why I sang you my song. To tell you I'd come and live with you in Camelot."

He shook his head. "Not in Camelot. In the real world. As my wife."

She closed her eyes momentarily and offered up a silent prayer of thanksgiving. When she opened them again, Michael was looking at her anxiously. "You will marry me, Blythe darling?"

"Of course I will." She smiled at him wistfully. "But I'll miss Camelot."

"We can visit, don't you think?"

She nodded, letting the smile that had been waiting break through. "We can visit."

"I think I will take that kiss back," he said abruptly, and he leaned to kiss her cheek, then murmured, "We can do better than this." His arms slipped around her and his mouth met hers.

All her senses soared. Although the office was too far away from the Starlight Room for her to hear Temptation playing, it seemed to her that she *could* hear music... loud brassy music for a carousel.

Michael ran his hands through her hair, gently, weighing it in his hands. Then he took her face between his hands and his lips met hers once more. Her tongue savored the sweetness and warmth of his mouth, and her hands moved lightly, possessively over his upper body under his jacket. She heard his breath quicken, and a moment later his hands slid down to first cup then stroke her breasts. She felt her nipples rise to his palms and pressed herself close to him, wanton in her need. Yet she felt none of the usual urgency that had always been between them and no regret that in a few minutes they would have to leave this quiet room. Soon they would go home together and undress. He would kiss the hollow of her throat, her shoulders, her breasts, until her fervor matched his own and they were both engulfed with a longing that demanded release. But there was no hurry now. They had a lifetime to love in.

Outside the office door someone laughed, and she became aware that people were nearby. But she couldn't bring herself to care. She wasn't thinking of the people out there at all. She wasn't worrying about Domingo, who must be waiting for her to return to her place on the stage. She was simply responding as passionately as she knew how to Michael's kisses and thinking that her glass unicorn would look just right on the mantel in Michael's house.

EXPERIENCE

Harlequin Temptation T.M.

ensuous...contemporary...compelling...reflecting today's love relationships! The passionate torment of a woman torn between two loves...the siren call of a career ...the magnetic advances of an impetuous employer–nothing is left unexplored in this romantic new series from Harlequin. You'll thrill to a candid new frankness as men and women seek to form lasting relationships in the face of temptations that threaten true love. *Don't miss a single one!* You can start new *Harlequin Temptation* coming to *your* home each month for just $1.75 per book–a saving of 20¢ off the suggested retail price of $1.95. Begin with your FREE copy of *First Impressions.* Mail the reply card today!

First Impressions
by Maris Soule

He was involved with her best friend! Tracy Dexter couldn't deny her attraction to her new boss. Mark Prescott looked more like a jet set playboy than a high school principal–and he acted like one, too. It wasn't right for Tracy to go out with him, not when her friend Rose had already staked a claim. It wasn't right, even though Mark's eyes were so persuasive, his kiss so probing and intense. Even though his hands scorched her body with a teasing, raging fire...and when he gently lowered her to the floor she couldn't find the words to say no.

word of warning to our regular readers: While Harlequin books are always in good taste, you'll find more sensuous writing in new *Harlequin Temptation* than in other Harlequin romance series.

™Trademarks of Harlequin Enterprises Ltd.

Exclusive Harlequin home subscriber benefits!

- SPECIAL LOW PRICES for home subscribers only
- CONVENIENCE of home delivery
- NO CHARGE for postage and handling
- FREE *Harlequin Romance Digest*®
- FREE BONUS books
- NEW TITLES 2 months ahead of retail
- MEMBER of the largest romance fiction book club in the world

---

GET FIRST IMPRESSIONS FREE
Harlequin Temptation™

Mail to: **HARLEQUIN READER SERVICE**

In the U.S.A. 2504 West Southern Avenue Tempe, AZ 85282	In Canada P.O. Box 2800, Postal Station 5170 Yonge Street, Willowdale, Ont. M2N 6J3

YES, please send me FREE and **without obligation** my *Harlequin Temptation* romance novel, *First Impressions.* If you do not hear from after I have examined my FREE book, please send me 4 new *Harlequin Temptation* novels each month as soon as they come off t press. I understand that I will be billed only $1.75 per book (total $7.00)–a saving of 20¢ off the suggested retail price of $1.95. The are no shipping and handling or any other hidden charges. There no minimum number of books that I have to purchase. In fact, I may cancel this arrangement at any time. *First Impressions* is mine keep as a free gift, even if I do not buy any additional books.

Name _____

Address _____ Apt. No. _____

City _____ State/Prov. _____ Zip/Postal Cod

Signature (If under 18, parent or guardian must sign.)

This offer is limited to one order per household and not valid to current *Harlequin Temptation* subscribers. We reserve the right to exercise discretion in granting membership.   142-BPX-MDCT
® ™ Trademarks of Harlequin Enterprises Ltd.   T-SUB-2US

If price changes are necessary you will be notified.

Offer expires May 31, 1985